Barriers

David F. Gray

Copyright 2022 for David F. Gray
Copyright 2022 for Red Cape Publishing

The characters and events in this book are fictitious. Any similarities to real persons, living or dead, is coincidental and not intended by the author.

Introduction

When I was in middle school (we called it Junior High back then) I was a part of a program that allowed students to buy paperback books relatively cheap. My parents indulged me and allowed me to buy several books a month. One of the covers in the catalogue that caught my eye featured a man with the head of a frog and dressed in the garb of an eighteenth-century gentleman. Over his head the title read 'The Shadow Over Innsmouth and Other Stories of Horror' by H.P. Lovecraft. I've loved ghost stories ever since I can remember and figured that this would be more of the same. I could not have been more wrong. The horrific and otherworldly images conjured by Lovecraft in those stories had a profound effect on my young imagination.

Many years later, as a young(ish) adult, I came across Stephen R. Lawhead's Pendragon Cycle, an amazing retelling of the Arthurian legend. At the time this consisted of three books: Taliesin, Merlin and Arthur. I became immersed in the lush world Lawhead painted with his words, so much so that I felt a real sense of loss and sadness when I finished them. I quickly moved on to Lawhead's Song of Albion, which I enjoyed even more than the Pendragon Cycle.

In his work, Lawhead delves deep into Celtic lore, including the Time Between Times, those transitional moments when it is neither day nor night, namely dawn and dusk. The ancient Celts believed that there was a deep mystery during these times, when the boundaries and barriers between the physical realm and spiritual realm were at their thinnest. I found the concept intriguing.

Lovecraft and Lawhead: other than the fact that both their last names start with an L, they could not be more different, but their collective work has had a major influence on my own. I have become fascinated with transitions, and the barriers between those transitions. There are the ordinary transitions we experience during our time on this planet: the transition between childhood and adulthood, between being single and married, the transition to parenthood, and many others.

The stories you are about to read deal with different types of transitions...and barriers. Here you will find fourteen tales that explore the transitions between the mundane and extraordinary, the natural and the supernatural, the real and the surreal. You will also encounter the barriers that lie at the threshold of these transitions. These barriers can protect us or imprison us. They can also be breeched, but that breeching is rarely a good thing.

My thanks to Peter and Leanne Blakey-Novis at Red Cape Publishing for making this collection possible. I would also like to thank Heidi, my beautiful wife of 37 years, for her constant support and belief. Finally, thanks to you, the reader, for investing a bit of your time in this collection. It is deeply appreciated.

Contents

Mark Is Still Missing	6
The Abomination of St. Jude	22
The Slave Canal	40
One Piece at a Time	50
The Call of Cats on a Pale Moon Night	64
The Bridge	73
Wade Flick	90
Mamaw's Beast	101
The Vampires Are Always Guilty	113
One Perfect Moment	124
The Cypress Wood Terror	140
The Running Shadows of Netherton's Peak	162
The Stars Denied	181
The Estate	197

Mark Is Still Missing

"Yeah, but I'm starting to get a little nervous."

I dreamed that on New Year's Eve, but it doesn't matter. It happened. I know, because the second time it wasn't a dream.

I'm making a mess of this, but that doesn't matter either. Last week, just as the knife slid in, I caught a glimpse of the blue house. For the first time in months, I actually have a chance...if I can get past *him*. I'm loading this document onto my computer because if...*when*...the barrier cracks, I'm going to push through it. If I don't make it back, I want someone to know what I've done and why.

You see, something took my son, and I'm going to take him back.

No parent should ever have to suffer the loss of a child, but it happens. Sickness, accidents, human monsters who prey on the young; sometimes, it just happens.

It happened to me.

God, it hurts to type that.

Mark, my twelve-year-old son and only child, disappeared six months ago, between one and three-fifteen on New Year's morning. The images that fill my mind are merciless and brutal. I see him caged like an animal for the amusement of some insane pedophile. Worse, I see him buried in a shallow grave, planted where no one will ever find him.

And those are the good days.

On the bad days, I think that something else has him, or almost has him. It's something so wrong that it cannot be conceived by the waking mind. It's all I can do to hang on to my sanity.

Jenny is not so lucky. My wife was the strongest person I have ever known, but losing Mark broke her. I visit her three times a week, but she no longer knows me. She doesn't know anyone. The pills she downed saw to that. She just lies in her bed, staring at something only she can see. The doctors try to offer some hope, but I can see the truth in their eyes. Jenny's mind is gone, buried deep in whatever world she's created for herself.

Even after all these months, I still remember every detail of the dream.

It's New Year's Eve. I have to work, but I'm going to meet Mark at a party at around two in the morning. In typical dream logic, some of my long-lost friends from high school will be there along with Mark's friends. I've made it a point to get each of them a gift certificate from a local restaurant.

I leave work and drive to the party. I'm a little concerned because it's in a bad neighborhood... drugs, gangs, and a crime rate that would make the south side of Chicago blush. It's also *my* neighborhood. God knows I've tried, but I've never been able to afford better.

I find the house and pull into the driveway. It's a tiny wooden number resting on concrete blocks. The white paint is faded and the entire structure tilts to the left. I go inside and find Mark sitting on a worn red couch watching television.

"How's the party?" I ask.

"Dull," he replies. "They're all asleep." I glance around and see that he's right. Everyone is sacked out

Barriers

on the floor, blankets pulled over their heads.

"Then let's go home," I say. Mark nods and we walk out of the house. My Mustang is still there in the driveway, but for some reason we decide to walk. It's a warm Florida night, so we go to the nearest intersection and take a left. Our house is maybe two miles away, but it's two miles through a bad neighborhood on the biggest party night of the year. We walk in silence, but suddenly I realize that I've forgotten to give my friends their gifts.

"Hang on a second," I tell Mark. "I'll be right back." I turn and trot back toward the old wooden house. Just like that, I abandon my son. But it's all right. It's just my dream, you see. Sometimes, we do things in our dreams that we would never do in waking life. At least, that's what I keep telling myself.

I get back to the house. This being a dream, I don't realize that it is now much larger, painted bright blue and two stories high. It is also on the other side of a street in what is now a much nicer neighborhood. I go inside, but everyone is still asleep. I leave the envelopes with the gift certificates on a table where my friends will find them and leave. Once outside, I see my Mustang sitting right where I left it. I suddenly realize I have left Mark alone. Pulling my phone out of my pocket, I hit the speed dial.

"It's me," I say when Mark answers. "Are you all right?"

"Yeah," he says, "but I'm starting to get a little nervous."

"Okay, hang on. I'm on my way back now." I get into my car and pull out of the driveway. When I get to the intersection, I see that the two-lane street has now

David F. Gray

become a busy four-lane highway. I pull out, make a left and hit the gas. I keep an eye peeled for Mark, but everything is different. Long, never ending strip malls line both sides of the highway. Their glaring neon lights make me squint so hard that I can't see the pavement. I stop the car and get out. I'm starting to get scared.

I must have made a wrong turn, I think. I leave my car sitting in the middle of the highway and start running back toward the house. The neon lights disappear but I keep running. Then, out of the darkness four figures appear. It's Jenny, along with her parents. The fact that my in-laws are both dead makes no difference. To my immense relief, Mark is with them.

"I've been looking for you," I say. Then I do a double take. The boy is not Mark. At least, he's not *my* Mark. He looks like Mark...sort of... but he's a good five years younger. "Where's Mark?" I ask, but Jenny ignores me. The four of them walk past me and disappear into the darkness. Suddenly I am terrified. Not only have I abandoned my son, but now I can't find my way back to him.

I make it back to the intersection and for an instant I see the tidy blue house. *I'll start from there,* I think, *and retrace my steps.* I turn the corner, but without any hint of transition, the house disappears. I can still see it, but even so, it's gone. Something has come between me and it...some kind of barrier. Far worse, there's something lurking within that barrier. I take a step forward, but the thing stirs. It sees me, and it *knows* me. I can't take it anymore. I flee.

I don't mean that I run. I flee.

I think that, at that moment, my waking mind decided that enough was enough. It took that dark dreamscape, crushed it into a tiny ball and hurled it deep into the recesses of my mind. I jerked awake and found myself lying in my own bed next to Jenny.

I glanced at my alarm clock and saw that it was three fifteen a.m. As in my dream, I had worked until well past midnight. Unlike my dream, there had been no party. Both Jenny and Mark had stayed home and watched the New Year come in on television. I lay there, heart pounding. After several minutes I couldn't stand it any longer. I slid out of bed, padded down the hall and peeked into Mark's room. His bed was empty. I stared at the tousled sheets.

He's in the bathroom, I thought, *or probably getting a drink of water in the kitchen.* But he was gone. The window in his bedroom was locked, and there was no sign of a struggle. He simply disappeared.

I don't remember much about that night. I ran about our tiny house like a madman for several minutes, convinced that Mark was somehow staying one step ahead of me. Finally, I woke Jenny. I told myself that she had let him stay overnight at a friend's house and had forgotten to tell me. The fact that I had looked in on him when I got home did not matter. My mind was grasping for any possible explanation. Jenny thought it was some kind of horrible joke, but gradually she realized that something was very wrong.

We called the police, of course. They searched the neighborhood but came up empty. Mark did not magically appear the next day, or the next week, or the next month. The police continued their investigation while Jenny and I slid deeper and deeper into our own private hell.

We didn't think things could get any worse, but after

a month, we discovered that we were now suspects in Mark's disappearance. The local news ran the entire story and suddenly we found ourselves huddling in the business end of a hurricane. Our friends deserted us and people at my job shunned me. That was it for Jenny. I came home one afternoon and found her lying on the floor, curled up with a pillow between her legs, staring into the distance. She's still staring.

After that, I moved through my day-to-day life like a dead man. Three months after Mark's disappearance, late one evening, I was again brought in for questioning. Bill Davis, the detective in charge, was on a mission. He was convinced of my guilt and nothing was going to sway him.

"Tell me exactly what you did when you discovered Mark's disappearance, Mr. Grant," he began. An hour later, he flat out accused me of murdering my son. "We've seen it a hundred times, Steve." He liked calling me Steve, even though I told him I preferred Steven. "A kid defies his father and the father lashes out in rage." He leaned across the interrogation table. His breath smelled of coffee and stale cigarettes. "You need help, Steve," he said. "I can get you that help. We can end this once and for all. Just tell me the truth and let me help you."

"I've told you the truth," I said, closing my eyes. "You just don't want to hear it." He growled, stood up and started the whole thing all over again. Five hours later, he stormed out of the room. I was released with a stern warning to not leave town.

A few days later, I was fired. Until last week, I spent my days staring at the walls of my house. The bills were coming due. We had always lived paycheck to

Barriers

paycheck, so I had maybe a month before the power and water got turned off. I didn't care. I wanted to die.

Then, eight days ago, my cell phone rang. It was around five in the afternoon and I had no intention of answering it, but the ring itself managed to penetrate the fog that had wrapped itself around my mind.

It was *Crazy Train*, by Ozzie Osborne, and it was Mark's ring. I pulled the phone out of my pocket and stared. Glowing in the twilight, Mark's picture stared back at me. In an instant, the mind-numbing terror and despair that had been my constant companions for six months vanished into nothingness. My heart soared. *He got away,* I cried silently. *Oh thank you God, he got away.* I hit the 'accept' button.

"Mark? MARK! Please let that be you!"

"Yeah, but I'm starting to get a little nervous." It was Mark's voice, and for a moment, that was all that mattered. Tears suddenly soaked my cheeks.

"Where are you? Just tell me where you are and I'll come and get you." For a moment, there was nothing. Then…

"I'm starting to get a little nervous." Now I actually listened. Mark's voice was dull…*pale.* It seemed to be coming from a long way away.

"Where are you?" I screamed. "For God's sake, just tell me where you are!" A loud clash of static made me wince, but I kept the phone to my ear. I heard Mark's voice again, but the static made it impossible to understand him.

"MARK! ANSWER ME!" The static grew worse, but finally I was able to make out four words.

"It's…dark…he's close." And the line went dead. I hit the redial button but the call did not go through.

David F. Gray

After several tries, I gave up and called Detective Davis. I could feel his disbelief as he listened.

"I think that your mind is trying to tell you to come here and confess," he said in that dull, flat professional tone that I had come to hate.

"You self-righteous bastard," I growled. "My son is out there. Now you get your fat, lazy ass in gear and find him, or so help me I'll…"

"You'll do nothing," snapped Davis. "You'll stay right where you are while I check this out." He hung up and called back a few hours later.

"No calls have been made to your cell phone, Steve," he practically crowed. "And your son's phone has not been used since his disappearance. Now, why don't you drop the act, come in and talk to me."

"Screw you," I snarled and hung up. I thumbed the 'menu' button on my phone but there was no record of Mark's call. My heart sank. *It's finally happening,* I thought. *Move over, Jenny. I'll be checking in soon.*

At that moment, my phone went off in my hand. It was *Crazy Train*, and the display clearly showed Mark's picture and name. At that instant, I wanted to slam it into the wall so hard that it would never ring again. I actually raised my hand to do just that, but of course, I couldn't. Instead, I thumbed the 'accept' tab and raised it to my ear.

"Mark?" My voice was a harsh whisper. I heard the sound of heavy breathing that seemed to go on forever. It sounded like someone running. "Mark," I pleaded. "Please son, talk to me. Where are you?" The panting stopped and was replaced by something much worse - weeping. It was Mark's voice. I was sure of it.

"Mark," I tried to say, but the name stuck in my

Barriers

throat. Suddenly I was sobbing, matching Mark breath for breath.

"Why...did...leave...me?" His voice was fading.

"I'm sorry," I said. It was almost impossible to breathe. "Oh dear God I am so sorry!"

"...I...can't...hear..." Those were Mark's last words to me. The line went dead and when I checked the menu, there was no record of his call. I threw it at the couch and fell to the floor, sobbing. I don't know how much time passed, but after a while I stopped crying. I lay there, eyes closed, hearing Mark's voice in my mind. *Why did you leave me?* It was a brutal accusation, but after a while I suddenly realized something. My eyes snapped open.

"Wait a minute," I croaked out loud. "I never left you." It was true, of course. When I came home from work on that terrible night, Mark was already in bed. I only abandoned him...

"In my dream," I whispered. It made no sense, and yet, it did. I sat up, thinking hard. I could feel my mind circling a truth...not a fact, but a truth. I think that it's something buried deep in all of us, something that we refuse to acknowledge. It has to do with that border... *barrier*... between asleep and awake. I think that that if we did manage to acknowledge it, it might drive us mad. It's an old truth...an ancient truth.

No, I won't write any more about that. Even here, at its fringe, I can feel the madness pushing at me, trying to get in. For Mark's sake, I can't allow that.

I had to do something, so I got in my car and headed deeper into the neighborhood. I had a rough idea of where the party house might be...the white one, not the blue one. I had never seen it of course, except in my dream, but I knew, or more accurately *felt*, where it might be. It was the illogical logic of dreams, but I was determined to search every street.

At first, it didn't work. There were a lot of decaying white houses, but none of them matched the party house. Night fell and darkness grew thick over the neighborhood. I pulled onto one of the narrow side streets and got out of my car. I reasoned that I had been on foot when I abandoned Mark, so maybe I needed to search on foot. It was a foolhardy thing to do, but I was exhausted and not thinking straight.

I don't think I realized it until I came to the next intersection. I paused at the stop sign and scanned the area. After a few seconds, I discovered a wonderful fact. I was excited. Against all odds, I was getting close. I could feel it. I took another long look at the surrounding houses, and suddenly the dark landscape in my dream began to match up with reality.

Oh my God, it's working, I thought. *I just have to find the way to go deeper in.* I didn't begin to understand what I was thinking and couldn't have cared less. I knew that if I could find the house, either the white one or the blue one, I could find Mark.

"You don't belong here," said a harsh voice. I whirled and came face to face with six dark figures. *I'm a dead man,* I thought. They were young, in their late teens. All of them were bigger than me, and all of them were armed. Four of them had wicked looking knives. The one in front held a sawed-off shotgun, while the final gang member held a massive pistol that was pointed straight at my head. "The way is closed," said the young man with the shotgun. "What's ours is ours, and what's his is his. This is ours." He spoke dull, flat

Barriers

English with no trace of an accent or any kind of 'street lingo'.

"Wait," I cried out, holding my hands up. "I just want…"

They rushed me. I turned and ran, but they caught me. What followed was brutal. They took turns. The ones with knives used them with surgical precision, inflicting dozens of shallow, painful cuts on my face, arms, legs and torso. The other two used their fists and feet. In minutes I was a bleeding, broken mess. I sank to the pavement, but 'shotgun boy' grabbed me by the scruff of the neck, yanked me to my feet and held me close. His breath reeked of dead things.

"What's his is his," he said again, "but sometimes he lets us have our fun." He grinned, and I think I screamed. For just an instant, I saw something reflected in his eyes. I don't remember what it was. I don't *want* to remember.

I caught a sudden movement off to my left. An instant later, I felt a searing hot pain in my right side as a knife slid between my ribs. Shotgun Boy let me go and I fell forward. Darkness pushed in on me and I started coughing up blood. *I'm sorry Mark,* I thought as the lights went out. Then, just before I lost consciousness, I saw it…the blue house. It was there, just a few lots away. I could see it, but more importantly, I could *sense* the white house hiding behind it. *I'm there,* I thought. *I found it.*

I saw something else as well - tentacles. There were dozens… hundreds… of them, and they were everywhere. Even in my barely conscious state, or perhaps because of it, I could see that they were infesting the neighborhood, straddling the street and winding through each and every house. Some were mere threads. Others were like gigantic pythons, throbbing with some kind of unimaginable power.

Six of them, each the width of a good-sized rattlesnake, were running straight to the gang members. I managed to raise my head. The tentacles ended at the base of each gang member's neck. Like their larger kin, they pulsed with some kind of dark obscene power.

My mind grew even darker, and as it did, the blue house shimmered and faded while the white house grew sharper. Behind the white house I sensed the portal. It was closed, but as I watched, it slowly opened. I tried to scream again, but only coughed up more blood. Standing in the opening to that gray land that existed between asleep and awake was a figure that...

No. I won't go there. That barrier between consciousness and unconsciousness exists for a reason, but there is something that lurks beyond that barrier that does not belong there. It is real. It is vile. It is beyond ancient.

I stared into the portal, past that...invader...that had no right to exist, and beyond it I could sense the countless screams of children who had been dragged into the darkness.

And one of those screams belonged to my son.

I reached out a hand, as if somehow I could reach into the portal and drag Mark back into my world, but that obscene creature blocked my feeble effort.

MINE. That single word blew past my fading senses, shattered my will and drove deep into my soul.

MINE. I could feel my last spark of life being crushed out of existence. The voice behind that word reeked of a power that existed before our universe was

Barriers

born.

MINE. The third time it spoke to me, it rammed a vision into my mind. I saw a near infinite web of portals that stretched throughout time and space, linking not only our dreams but the dreams of billions of other races on billions of other worlds. I could sense life energy flowing out of those dreams and into the thing inside the portal. I could see it as it squatted in the center, a bloated spider gorging itself on its prey.

MINE. For the final time it spoke, this rapist of dreams. I could feel my very essence being compressed into a tiny, fading spark, soon to be extinguished. Then the vision faded. The portal disappeared, along with the white house. I was back on the street, surrounded by the gang. Standing above me, Shotgun Boy grinned again.

"What's his is his, and what's ours is ours." I thought of the tentacle burrowing into the back of his neck and understood just how wrong he was.

"You're…all…his," I managed to croak. Then a booted foot smashed against my face. My last thought was a rerun. *I am a dead man.*

As it turned out, I was wrong. Someone called the police. They were on scene in two minutes. The paramedics arrived almost at the same time. The gang fled, melting into the neighborhood. I was rushed to the nearest hospital. After six hours of emergency surgery, I stabilized. The knife thrust had not been fatal, and while the cuts were plentiful, they were not life threatening. I spent a day and a night in intensive care, another day in recovery and the next five days in a semi-private room, thanks to the fact that my insurance was still in effect. Yesterday I was discharged. The doctors all say that I'm lucky to be alive. I can't argue the point, but it's irrelevant

I know where Mark is, and I'm going to get him back.

There's so much I don't understand, but I do know one damning fact: The creature that took Mark did not come through my son's dream, it came through *mine*. Which means it's my fault. If I had not abandoned him in the dream, he would be safe with me today. Insane? Maybe, but it's the truth.

Here's another truth. Mark is still out there. Maybe he's managed to somehow stay free. I don't know that... my phone has been silent...but I have to hope. It's all I've got.

It's late now, well past midnight. It's still agony to move. I'm not even close to full strength, but I don't care. I'm going out again.

A moment ago, I peeked through my bedroom window. The street was quiet and the houses were dark. A single streetlight painted everything in harsh, amber tones. All seemed normal, but then I let my eyes defocus and wander. The neighbor's hedge rustled in a certain way, and the oak tree in my yard creaked and bent. In my mind, I saw tentacles. I shuddered at the idea that they may very well be infesting my home.

What's his is his. I don't know why *he* chose this God-forsaken neighborhood, but I am certain that he's watching me, waiting for me to make another try for Mark.

I'm not going to disappoint him. That vision he sent me might have been his way of saying that getting my son back was impossible, but I don't care. Tonight I'm heading deep into the neighborhood. I'm going to keep prodding and poking. That barrier is old. Maybe the

Barriers

portal isn't the only way in. Maybe there is a crack somewhere that I can squeeze through.

Also, whatever it is that took Mark is old beyond old, and more often than not, the old are also frail, even senile. A fool's hope? Maybe, but it's all I have. If I can find a way in, then maybe I'll have a chance. If not, well, at least I'll know that I tried. I won't abandon Mark... never again.

I can't think of anything else. I'm going to e-mail this document to that fool Davis. I have no doubt that he'll have a bed ready for me next to Jenny as soon as he reads it. It doesn't matter. If I can bring Mark out, all will be forgiven. If not, then I won't be coming back.

Something rustles outside my window. Maybe it's a stray cat, but I don't think so. I'm out of time.

I love you Jenny. I always have, and I always will.

Hang on Mark. I'm coming.

* * *

Memo: To Captain Rachel Ferguson
From: Det. William Davis
RE: Case MP-TPA-1104, Grant, Mark
Boss:
Here's a copy of Steven Grant's e-mail. According to the time stamp, it was sent just hours before his disappearance yesterday. Forensics has confirmed that it was sent from his computer. As you can see, he is deeply disturbed.

I am now certain that Grant was responsible for the disappearance of his son, Mark. We've distributed his picture to every local and federal agency, so I doubt he'll be able to elude us for long. As for his son, well, I've got a bad feeling that if we ever do find him, it will be in a shallow grave in an abandoned lot somewhere in his neighborhood.

On a personal note, I take full responsibility for Steven Grant's disappearance. I didn't think he had the guts to run. If you let me keep the case, I won't rest until I find this bastard. You've got my word on that.

Regards,
Bill.

Barriers

The Abomination of St. Jude

The street cleaner rumbled down Spruce Avenue, its spinning brushes throwing up tiny tornadoes of grime and soot. The miniature vortexes whipped across the cement, tearing at the legs of the only person who dared brave the dreary weather. This solitary figure trudged along the sidewalk, shoulders hunched against the drizzling October rain.

Destin Phillips pulled his raincoat tighter around his chest and silently cursed the hulking machine as it soiled the pants of one of his few remaining decent suits. The machine's operator, perched on his seat high above the world, ignored Destin's discomfort, his attention focused on the empty street. The cleaner trundled onward, disappearing around the corner less than a block away.

It was well past two in the morning. Destin had been walking the dark Cincinnati streets for almost six hours, with only the widely spaced amber streetlights to guide him. He did not know what else to do. Every now and then he would reach into his coat pocket and grab the crumpled sheet of paper he had stuffed there earlier that afternoon. The instant he touched it, his face would go slack and his eyes would glaze over. He had known it was coming...had expected it, in fact, but the harsh reality of its physical presence felt like a knife corkscrewing into his gut.

This is to inform you that the Federal Bureau of Investigation has instigated proceedings against you, stemming from accusations of insider trading. Pursuant to an agreement reached with your firm, you will be allowed to surrender yourself on the first of November, 2021. Failure to do so will result in additional charges. There was more...much more, but it all boiled down to one simple fact. Everything he had worked for was gone. One brief lapse in judgment and now, at the relatively young age of thirty-six, he was an outcast. He was tempted to find a hand bell and ring it as he walked, all the while crying out 'Unclean!'

His was nearing the final stages of exhaustion. He took another step forward, but the toe of his expensive dress shoe caught on an uneven place in the sidewalk. With a startled cry he tumbled forward. His outstretched hands slammed into the rough concrete, sending jolts of pain coursing through his arms. His knees hit an instant later, and he felt the flimsy material of his suit pants give way. A wave of nausea rolled through his stomach.

Suddenly the dam he had constructed in his mind to keep the day's events at bay gave way. He knelt there on the sidewalk and discovered one simple, crushing fact. He did not have the will to get up. He had not eaten since early that morning. That, coupled with his never-ending walk, had pushed him to his physical and mental limits. At that moment, all he wanted to do was roll over and die. Instead, he managed to crawl away from the street on all fours. He desperately needed to rest.

He made it to the edge of the sidewalk and was somewhat surprised to find a wide set of smooth concrete steps waiting for him. Looking up into the drizzling rain, he saw that he had fallen in front of a massive church. He grimaced at the irony. *Great,* he thought, raising his eyes to the black, starless sky.

Barriers

Where were you six months ago? Since he had never really believed in God, he did not expect an answer. He was not disappointed.

The building was huge, more of a cathedral than a simple gathering place. Four wide marble columns supported an ornate roof that ended high above in a long tapering steeple. The structure itself seemed to be made of large, rectangular granite blocks, each the size of a small car. The two sets of dark wooden doors at the top of the steps looked sturdy enough to withstand a determined siege. The steeple was lit with a glaring spotlight, and there were five smaller lights inset into the granite above the doors. On a cornerstone to his right, etched deeply into the weathered stone, were the words 'The Church of Saint Jude'.

Moving in slow motion, he slid up onto the first step and rolled into a sitting position. Wrapping his arms around his aching knees, he let his head sink down onto his chest. He sat there, unmoving, a poster child for utter defeat.

His thoughts were hazy and indistinct. He knew that he should go home, but lacked the will even to stand. There was no one there anyway...had not been, in fact, for over a year. Carrie and the kids had gone to live with her parents in Oklahoma, and he was lucky if he heard from them every other week. The courts had sided with her. The first time he had cheated on her, he had promised that he would never do it again. After the third time, Carrie had simply packed her bags and left, with both Alan and Nikki in tow.

"I've seen some hard luck cases in my time, but I think that I might just be looking at a new standard for misery." Destin's thoughts were so muddy that it took him several seconds to realize someone had just spoken to him. He raised his head and saw the priest sitting next to him on his right, regarding him with bemused pity.

"Huh?" It was the best that he could do. He had been so wrapped up in his own troubles that he had not heard the other man approach. He blinked, trying to clear his head.

"If I were to hazard a guess," continued the priest, "I'd say that you've probably lost your job or your family. Both, maybe?" He paused expectantly, waiting for an answer. He was an older man, with close-cropped gray hair and a football lineman's build. His voice was a rumbling bass, so deep that Destin suddenly envisioned him wearing a striped vest, sporting a handlebar mustache and belting out "Lyda Rose" in a barbershop quartet.

"Uh." Destin tried again but did not have the words.

"It's okay. Believe me when I tell you that you're not alone." The priest smiled and held out a hand. "I'm Max. Max Sloan, the pastor here." Destin's hand moved automatically. Sloan's grip was firm and warm.

"Destin," he replied. It felt as if his mouth was filled with cotton balls. He swallowed and tried again. "Destin Phillips. It's nice to meet you, Father." Sloan smiled again.

"Destin. That's nice, like destiny. Oh, and I'm not a priest, just a humble layman." Destin glanced down at Sloan's clothes. The man certainly looked the part of a Catholic priest. He was wearing the traditional white collar, black coat, shirt and pants. Sloan shrugged.

"My people like it better if I wear the outfit. They seem to find some comfort in it." He nodded toward the doors. "Why don't you come inside for a while?" Destin shook his head.

"I'm not Catholic," he said. "I'm not much of anything, for that matter." Sloan laughed.

"Neither am I," he answered. "My church is something of an anomaly. We don't belong to any particular denomination, and we certainly don't worship any kind of traditional god." He gestured toward the building. "St. Jude was closed and deconsecrated years ago. We just use the place and pay a little rent. Sooner or later the Diocese will probably start a new congregation here, but until then, it's our home." He nodded at the doors again. "Come on in. At least you can get out of this wretched drizzle for a while. I can even offer you a hot cup of coffee." Again, Destin hesitated. Then a wave of exhaustion washed over him and he sagged in on himself.

"For a little while, I guess," he mumbled. Sloan stood, smiling. With a tremendous effort, Destin lurched to his feet. He found himself looking up at Sloan and suddenly realized that he was standing next to a very big man. At six feet even, Destin was not exactly short, but Sloan topped him by at least another four or five inches.

With a nod, the reverend turned and marched up the steps. Destin followed obediently. He felt nothing...neither relief nor anxiety. He just wanted to sleep and forget about this entire wretched day.

Sloan reached the double doors on the right and pulled them open with ease. Destin stepped inside and found himself in a rather ornate, if small, vestibule. The odor common to most older churches... stale air, flowers and Pine Sol...settled over him. For a moment,

David F. Gray

it was almost suffocating, and he had to resist the desire walk out. Then his sense of smell adjusted and he relaxed. Dark oak paneling lined the walls, and thick blue carpet covered the floor.

It should have felt warm and inviting, but to Destin it was rather claustrophobic. Still, it was warm, and that was enough. While the Ohio fall was mild this year, wandering the streets in the forty-degree cold, hour after hour, had been enough to chill him to the bone.

Taking off his raincoat, he followed Sloan through a swinging wooden door, this one much less intimidating than the main doors, and found himself in the sanctuary. The claustrophobia disappeared and he took a deep breath. His mind cleared a little.

"This is something," he murmured. Sloan nodded.

"It was built over a century ago," he said. "Most of the decor is original...the pews, the woodwork, the stained glass. We cleaned it up when we moved in, but it was already in pretty good shape. It's surprising that the Diocese would let all this just sit, but they've been having some pretty serious money troubles, among other things." Destin nodded absently.

The sanctuary was big enough to seat at least five hundred people. Two rows of dark wooden pews ran all the way to the front, lined up in neat formation and forming a left, right and center aisle. Overhead, the vaulted ceiling disappeared into the shadows. Six golden chandeliers, each at least ten feet in diameter and hanging on long chains, bathed the entire area in a soft, golden light. The altar stood on a raised platform and was covered with dark, expensive looking wood. The walls on either side featured tall, rectangular stained-glass windows that ran from floor to ceiling. It was too dark to make out any details, but Destin assumed that, like any other church, they depicted various biblical scenes.

The wall behind the altar featured a stained-glass window of another sort. It was artificially lit from behind, shining down on the altar and bathing it in a surreal glow. The glass was cut in irregular shapes that formed a sort of abstract, multicolored vortex. The interlocking swirls glowed with vivid reds, blues, greens and a hundred other rich hues. He stared at the pattern, his eyes following the different lines.

"It does demand your attention, doesn't it," chuckled Sloan. "Don't bother trying to make sense out of it. You'll give yourself a headache."

"Too late," muttered Destin. He blinked his eyes, suddenly dizzy. He swayed and would have fallen if Sloan had not caught him.

"Over here." Sloan led him to the center aisle and nodded at the nearest pew. "It's wide enough so that you won't fall off the edge. I'll get you that coffee and then you can rest for a while. Okay?" Destin did not have the strength to argue. He lay stomach down on the hard wood of the pew and cradled his head in his arms. The exhaustion he had held at bay finally breached his defenses and he sank into a deep, dreamless sleep.

***

He was awakened sometime later by the murmur of several low voices. At first, he thought he was dreaming, but as he slowly regained consciousness he began to realize that he was not alone. For several seconds, he did not remember where he was. Then his brain revved up to full speed and his thoughts sorted themselves into their proper order.

He groaned as the harsh reality of his life reasserted itself and he glanced at his watch. His eyes were watering, causing the tiny digital numbers to blur in the dim light. He blinked, clearing them, and saw that it was barely after four in the morning. He had been asleep for less than two hours. He let his head sink back down onto the pew, thinking that he had at least several more hours before he would be forced to face this day, which would certainly be worse than the preceding one. Then the voices reasserted themselves into his consciousness. *Huh?* Slowly he pushed himself up high enough to peek over the pew in front of him.

At the front of the sanctuary, a group of about thirty people were gathered. They were seated in the first row of pews and looked rather lost in the huge space. Destin started to sit all the way up, but then froze. What were these people doing here at this hour? Sloan had called his congregation an anomaly, but this was just a little *too* weird. Wanting suddenly to be anywhere else, Destin lowered his head again, intending to crawl between the pews to the aisle and slip out the main entrance.

"Rabba, sabbac. Rabba sabbac. Ra-ba-ba-ba-ba. Neidi an dre robo sabbacc." The nonsense words boomed out through the sanctuary, and Destin's gut clenched. The deep voice was coming from *behind* him. He twisted around in time to see Max Sloan, now clad in a full- length vestment of pure red, stride past him. His right hand was raised as if in blessing, and in his left he carried a long, polished staff tipped with a brass knob. The reverend did not so much as glance in his direction, but Destin suddenly felt exposed...naked. Sloan continued on toward the front of the sanctuary, all the while chanting his nonsense words.

Even with his limited knowledge of religious practices, Destin understood that the reverend was speaking in tongues. Over a year ago, before Carrie had walked out, he had been channel surfing in the middle of the night and caught the tail end of a program that featured a very energetic televangelist. The man had whipped his crowd of followers into a frenzy, chanting the same type of nonsense words. Sloan reached the front of the sanctuary and, as he turned to face his tiny flock, he switched to English.

"We call upon you, our great and terrible god, who was alive, is now dead, and will soon live again. We call upon you, who dwells dreaming in the hidden city. We call upon you, O Great Old One, whose world this was and shall be again. We beseech you, our savior from the Devourer of the Universe. Grant us your vision. Allow us to see what is to come through the vessel you have sent."

Sloan fell silent and Destin shivered with fear. There was an atmosphere of what he could only describe as deadly expectation permeating the sanctuary. It was as real as the pew beneath him. It pressed in on him from all directions, as if trying to crush him into a tiny, insignificant speck of dust. The very air around him felt stale, lifeless...*ancient*.

Fighting his growing panic, he slid off the pew and crouched on all fours. Gathering his nerve, he crawled over to the aisle. He peeked out from between the pews, half expecting to see Sloan crouching there, ready to grab him and drag him kicking and screaming to the

David F. Gray

front, but the center aisle was empty.

Fighting the urge to bolt, he crouched low and dashed through the back doors. Once in the vestibule, he stood up straight and almost leaped to the main entrance. He threw himself against the door closest to him, and nearly screamed when it did not move. He pushed again but it barely rattled. Panicked, he grabbed the long iron handle that was bolted to the door and pulled, but again the door did not budge. He tried the other doors in quick succession with the same result. He frantically looked for a lock or dead bolt, but there was nothing. Behind him, he could hear the chanting gathering both speed and volume. His eyes darted around the vestibule, but there was no other way out.

Suddenly the chanting stopped. Destin froze, straining his ears. He was effectively trapped, because he knew that no matter what happened, he did not dare go back into the sanctuary. Seconds dragged by. Then another sound, muted and dull but still all too audible, came from behind the swinging doors.

The scream that he had managed to suppress burst out of his lungs. He slammed his shoulder into the nearest door, planted his feet against the carpet and pushed with every fiber of his being. The doors groaned but did not give. The sound grew louder and Destin screamed again. It seemed to penetrate deep into both his body and mind. He had no reference, no way to compare it to anything in the encyclopedia of his memory. It crawled, and it slithered, but it also clicked and rolled. It walked on two feet, and four, and a thousand. It did all of these things, and none of them. It was vile, and it was alien, but a part of him, a very old, ancient, *buried* part, recognized it and sent one single word crashing into his conscious mind...*run*. He swung around, jamming his back against the door. At that instant, one of the swinging doors rocked slightly.

"Please," he managed to croak. His throat was dry and even that single word caused him to cough. The door rattled again and then slowly swung open. His eyes looked into the darkness beyond the door. They saw what lurked there, but his mind rebelled. It simply refused to process the signal it was getting. Instead, it flicked a switch and shut itself down. Destin tumbled forward, unconscious before he hit the floor.

***

Do not wake up.
Do not wake up.
For the love of God, do not wake up!

For the remainder of his short life, Destin would never be sure if someone was whispering those words to him or if his own mind was begging him to remain unconscious. He struggled, trying to move, but something bound him. He tried to breathe, but something clogged his throat. Terror overrode reason and he flailed against his bonds. They tightened, and he struggled harder. Darkness closed in but he fought it, until finally a tiny speck of light flared.

Reaching out with his mind, he grabbed the light and squeezed. The light flared brighter and the darkness retreated. Destin fixed every ounce of his strength on the growing light. He suddenly understood that he was still unconscious, just as he understood that if he did not somehow manage to break free of his bonds, he would never wake up. He struggled harder, until finally the dark force that was imprisoning him shattered. He opened his eyes.

And wished to God that he had obeyed the order to stay unconscious.

He was lying on a hard, cold surface. Above him a large, golden chandelier glowed softly. His memory rebooted and he understood that he was lying on the altar in the deconsecrated Church of St. Jude. Somewhere to his left, he heard a low murmur. He moved his arms and legs, surprised to find that he was not bound. He turned his head, half expecting Max Sloan to pop into his field of vision wielding some kind of sacrificial knife. Sloan was indeed there, flanked by his congregation. They were several feet away and below him, on the main floor. The pastor, at least, appeared to be unarmed. His staff was nowhere to be seen. His eyes met Destin's and he smiled. He glanced at his followers.

"See? He's strong. Our master chose well." Several of the congregants nodded.

"Wha..." The instant Destin tried to speak, his dry throat rebelled and he began to cough. Sloan held out a hand and someone handed him a glass of water. He climbed the two steps to the main platform and held it out to Destin. Destin leaned away, shaking his head.

"It's just water, Destin," said Sloan. "Believe me, if we wanted you dead, you would be dead. Please, drink. You're badly dehydrated." Destin coughed again. He sat up and out of desperation took the water. It was warm but at least it seemed to be pure. He drank it down and Sloan deftly retrieved the glass. A woman, short, stocky with bleached blonde hair, moved to his side and took it. With a neutral glance at Destin, she

Barriers

rejoined the congregation. Destin looked at Sloan.

"I'm going to leave now," he managed to say, although his voice was still raspy. Sloan smiled again.

"You have no idea how much I envy you," he said. "What you are going to see..." He shook his head. "I would gladly consign my soul to oblivion for just a glimpse." Moving slowly, Destin swung his legs off the altar. He started to stand, but something grabbed him from behind. With a startled cry he fell backward, his head hitting the unyielding stone of the altar. Darkness flitted around the edge of his vision. He struggled, but whatever was holding him easily resisted his effort.

"Let...me...go," he gasped. He lunged forward, trying to roll off the altar, but was immediately pulled back. His body was forced flat onto the hard surface, both arms and legs immobilized. His head thrashed back and forth, trying to get a glimpse of what was assaulting him, but could see nothing. "What...what..."

"You beheld the servant of the One We Do Not Name," said Sloan. His voice seemed to come from a great distance. "It led you here, and when you saw it in the foyer, it nearly destroyed you. Now, your mind refuses to allow you to see it, but don't worry, Destin. Soon, you will witness signs and wonders. Your mind will open and you will be forever changed. Oh, how I envy you!"

Something wrapped itself around Destin's head and clamped his mouth shut. He wanted to beg Sloan to release him. He wanted to find Carrie and beg her to forgive him. He wanted to surrender himself to the F.B.I. and atone for his crimes. He wanted to forget the creeping, growing terror that held him in an unbreakable grip. He wanted to...

Something...something cold and hot and wet and dry and oozing...pressed against his left temple. He moaned and tried to pull away, but it pressed harder. He screamed a silent scream as the pressure increased. Then, something gave way. It wasn't skin or bone. His skull did not cave in, nor did he bleed. Some kind of natural, ancient defense that Destin possessed...that all humanity possessed...disintegrated. His mind was left open and vulnerable.

He was invaded.

Above him the cathedral ceiling of the church dissolved like sugar in water. Beyond was a field of stars, billions upon billions of blazing stars. He felt his mind, perhaps even his soul, lifted. He fell toward the stars until suddenly he was swimming through them. For an eternal moment, his terror disappeared, replaced by pure wonder. Faster and faster he swan, until the stars disappeared. Now he existed in absolute darkness.

You have passed beyond the veil of time and space. Sloan's voice echoed all around him as if it was the voice of God, but Destin retained just enough of his reason to understand that his body was still on the granite altar and he was hearing Sloan through his physical ears.

You are retracing the path of the One We Do Not Name. It came here with its brothers when our world was ever so young, and man was nothing more than a distant dream. It had been driven across the stars by its great enemy and needed refuge. In time, its brothers left and returned to fight. Now the time of our god is near. It feeds to grow strong, but it is not unkind. It takes from you, but it gives so much in return. Look, Destin. Look and see the wonders!

Barriers

Far ahead, a tiny spark of light flickered. Destin felt his speed increase and he flew toward it with a velocity that was beyond thought. It grew and took the shape of a great, sparkling pinwheel, and he understood that he was seeing an entire galaxy of stars. He slowed and came to a full stop. The galaxy rose above him, like a coin standing on its edge, incomprehensible in its size.

Then Destin's perspective changed and he understood that everything he knew, everything he believed, was wrong. Against his will, his vision was forced closer to that shining center. He did not see, for he had no eyes, but he perceived. Then mercilessly, his vision was forced beyond the galaxy, to the darkness beyond, to...

NO!

He wanted to shut it out, but contrary to what Sloan said, the power that imprisoned him knew nothing of compassion or pity. He was forced to look, just as he was forced to understand. Then, mercifully, all went dark. He struggled and discovered that he could move again. He opened his eyes.

He was still lying on the altar, but now the sanctuary was much brighter. He tried to turn his head and found that it was no longer bound. He looked to his right and saw daylight streaming through the stained-glass windows. He flexed his arms and legs and then slowly rolled over and sat up. The sanctuary was empty. Sloan and his congregation were nowhere to be seen. Destin put his feet on the floor and stood.

"You saw." The voice came from the rear of the sanctuary. Destin blinked and saw Sloan coming through the inner door. "You understand now."

"I understand," said Destin. His voice was flat and

lifeless. "But you don't." Sloan smiled and walked toward him. Destin watched as the big man approached. He no longer feared the pastor. He no longer feared anything. Fear is predicated on caring, and he knew that he would never care about anything again.

"They all say that," said Sloan as he reached the steps of the altar. "It's a normal reaction. You've seen eternity, Destin. You've seen the truth!"

"Yeah," said Destin. "I've seen the truth." He stepped down off the platform, wobbled slightly, and then walked past Sloan as if he did not exist. The pastor made no effort to stop him.

"I truly envy you," said Sloan. "I wish I could see..."

"No," said Destin, whirling on him. "You really don't." He took a step toward the pastor. "You're right, I saw the truth, and the truth is, we don't matter. Nothing matters. Do you get that? Nothing we do, nothing we have ever done, nothing our entire race has ever done, matters." Sloan shook his head, smiling.

"The One We Do Not..." he began.

"Your god feeds," said Destin. "That's all it does. It feeds on us so that it can grow strong enough to return to its war."

"But look at what it gives us in return," said Sloan.

"An accident," said Destin. "It forges a connection with its food, but it's nothing more than a byproduct of its feeding."

"But what you saw," said Sloan. "Don't you understand, Destin? You saw things that the rest of us dare not even dream about."

"I SAW YOUR GOD'S ENEMY," screamed Destin. The sudden release of rage caused him to wobble again and he quickly composed himself. "I thought it was a

Barriers

galaxy, but it was a...a thing. I looked into its center, and the center was an eye. Do you understand? This thing is as big as a galaxy and it's alive."

"Magnificent," whispered Sloan. "We have brought in many others, but no one has gone as far as you. No one has ever seen the Enemy. I had no idea."

"You still don't," said Destin. "What I saw was just a foot soldier. One of *billions*. There's something else beyond it...something bigger than all the soldiers combined, and that is what is giving the orders. It's beyond your comprehension, *reverend*." He forced the corners of his mouth into a very slight smile, although there was no emotion behind it. "You're not capable of comprehending it." For the first time a hint of anger crossed Sloan's face.

"Be careful," he warned.

"Or what?" said Destin. "You'll kill me? Don't make me laugh. Your god fed on me. It's still feeding on me, and trust me, the last thing you want to do is deprive it of its food." He turned his back on Sloan. "Goodbye, reverend. You have my pity." He walked away, knowing that Sloan would not stop him.

He could feel his connection with Sloan's god. It was as if some vile tentacle had fastened itself to the base of his skull. It followed him, stretching back to the pocket of un-reality with which the god's servant cloaked itself. He could almost see billions of other tentacles running throughout both time and space, all ending at a hidden city beneath a dark ocean. No matter where he went, not matter how far he ran, that tentacle would follow him for the rest of his life. He would not even be allowed the mercy of madness. Sloan's unnamed god liked its food sane.

***

A hearing gave way to a trial. His firm abandoned him, his former bosses sacrificing him in order to save themselves. They did not offer him legal representation, and Destin would have refused even if they had offered. He would not even allow the state to provide him with an attorney. He stood mute at his trial, offering no defense.

The judge was in no mood to show leniency. It was an election year and she was in a tight race. She sentenced Destin to fifteen years in the Ohio State Penitentiary. If he behaved himself, he would be out in seven. He was taken into custody, processed and incarcerated.

Less than a year later, he was found dead in his cell. The autopsy was performed by the prison doctor and caused a bit of a stir. While Destin Phillips retained the appearance of a man in his thirties, his organs were aged, withered and blackened. The report was examined and re-examined, until it was finally buried and forgotten.

Barriers

The Slave Canal

The water gurgles. It's a nauseating sound, like mucus sliding down a sick man's throat. There's no breeze and the heavy, humid air is suffocating. Judging from the dull orange sun hanging just above the trees, I've got maybe thirty minutes of light left. After that…

Sinkholes…got to remember the sinkholes.

My name is Tobias Franklin Gamble, Toby to my friends. I am… was…a professor of archeology at the University of Florida. A few years back, I scored a lucrative research grant from a private foundation interested in Florida Civil War history. This was due, in part, to my family tree. It turns out that one of my ancestors, John Gamble, owned a sprawling plantation in central Florida during the mid-nineteenth century. It was he who commissioned the digging of what would become known as the Slave Canal. He and his fellow plantation owners wanted a short cut between the Wacissia and Aucilla rivers in order to get their cotton to market faster.

Now that I'm here, floating in the actual canal, I can only imagine the agony his slaves must have endured digging it by hand. How many of them died here, left to rot in the water? That's a rhetorical question, by the way. I already know.

The canal was a spectacular failure. It was too shallow. The cotton barges kept getting stuck on the bottom. They would have to be unloaded, pushed until they floated free again, and reloaded. In addition, branches from the overhanging trees would fall on a regular basis and would have to be cleared away. The resulting delays ended up being far more costly than the old route.

Outside forces played a role in the canal's demise as well. A few years after it was dug, the railroad arrived, providing a much faster way to transport the cotton. Not long after that, the Civil War ended slavery, in theory at least.

The digging of the canal marked the beginning of John Gamble's personal demise, and the war completed it. He was ruined financially and it was said that he died a broken man. The canal was abandoned but it survived. It's still there, waiting for anyone who has the patience to find it. It runs about two and a half miles and is only thirty feet across at its widest point. In some places it's barely a foot deep, but it can be easily traveled by canoe.

A few years ago, some low-level bureaucrat in Tallahassee got the notion that the name Slave Canal was offensive and launched a campaign to change it. He thought that Cotton Run Canal was a much better name. He might have succeeded, but he had not counted on the stiff resistance from the local residents, both black and white. The Slave Canal was a part of their heritage, and they felt that to rename it dishonored the lives of the slaves who labored in such agonizing conditions to dig it.

I've never had the desire to see it. As far as I'm concerned, that part of my family history is best forgotten, but I had taken the foundation's money and I owed them at least one properly researched paper on the subject. I spent weeks combing through the university archives, finding a few tidbits of the canal's history. Then I turned to the social media sites and

Barriers

fared a little better. Although there wasn't a great deal of the canal's history available, there were plenty of pictures of the canal itself. It turns out that it has a small but avid group of regular visitors.

After that, my research hit a wall, so I decided to paddle the canal for a day and see if I could find some inspiration. Then I would dig through my family archives. Correction: I would dig through my family junk, stored away in my attic. I doubted that I would find anything useful, but it was worth a try. And so, a few days ago I packed some food in a knapsack, rented a canoe and set out on my grand adventure.

The canal is not easy to find. There's no sign saying, 'SLAVE CANAL HERE'. The entrance is clogged with vegetation and practically invisible from the main river. I launched my canoe in the morning but did not find the canal until just before noon. I mentioned that it is a favorite for a small group of travelers, but they usually come during the summer. Since it was late September, no one was around. I found the entrance and pushed through.

How can I begin to describe such beauty? The banks are covered with lush green undergrowth accented with red, blue and yellow wildflowers. Spanish moss dangles from the trees that line both sides of the canal. The branches intersect above, filtering the sunlight into a soft yellow haze. The pristine water is fed continuously by crystal clear springs.

I got in but I couldn't get out. Am I getting ahead of myself? Probably, but my time is growing short. I spent the day navigating the canal, but when it was time to go home, I discovered that I was lost. Understand; the canal is only two and a half miles long and runs in a relatively straight line. There are no mazelike passages, just a single thoroughfare. I paddled to the other end, turned around and came back.

I found the entrance that led to the Wacissia River, but when I tried to get through the foliage, my canoe got stuck. I backed off and tried again with the same result. I got frustrated and tried again, ramming the canoe forward as hard as I could, but once more I was repulsed. I backed off and sat there, gasping for air, feeling both disoriented and a little frightened.

I can't really explain it, and I don't have the time anyway, but somehow the way out had become closed, at least to me. I could see the entrance. For that matter, I could see the river beyond, but I could not get out. I made another attempt, paddling as hard as I could, but failed. Leaving my backpack in the canoe, I levered myself over the edge into the warm water. It was barely waist high, but even so, I could not push the canoe through the entrance. In desperation I abandoned the canoe and tried to force my way through, but I still could not get out. It was as if some kind of barrier, both real and yet not real, had been placed across the entrance. As absurd as it sounds, I was trapped.

That was three days ago. I didn't give up, but the harder I tried to escape, the more confusing everything got. I could *feel* the way out. I knew it was there, but I could not penetrate the barrier.

On my first full day in the canal, I beached the canoe and tried to get out on foot. I spent hours walking in circles. Yesterday I tried the water again. Somewhere around noon I felt the barrier waver. For a brief moment I sensed the way out. I forced the canoe forward, but it closed before I could escape. I paddled

Barriers

to the other end only to be met with the same result.

The sun set and darkness fell over the canal, marking the end of my second day. I pulled the canoe onto the bank and tried to think, but it was hard to concentrate. I was a creature of academia. A visit to the campus gym three times a week was the extent of my physical conditioning. I was exhausted and my thoughts were muddled and unfocused. I was nearly out of food and drinkable water. I understood that if I could not find a way out in the next few days, I could most likely die in the canal that was commissioned by my ancestor and dug by his slaves. I drew my knees up to my chin, laid my head on them and faded into a light, uneasy sleep.

Someone screamed. Someone else joined them. I was jolted out of my doze so hard that I would have would have overturned the canoe if I had not beached it. I blinked my eyes and tried to clear my head. The screaming grew louder as others, many others, joined in.

I came to full awareness and saw the light. It was everywhere. No, that's wrong. The sky was dark, and so was the land. The light was coming from the water. It was a sickly, brutal, *obscene* green. I could see that the light, and the screams, seemed to emanate from the center of the canal.

Those screams...

They were the screams of those who had abandoned all hope of salvation. They were the screams of those doomed to unending torment. They were the screams of the damned. I scrambled to my feet and turned to run. Of course, there was nowhere to run, but the thought of stumbling blindly through the dense forest in the middle of the night was preferable to being near the water.

It didn't matter. Even as I tried to escape, something snaked out of the light and took hold of me. I could not see anything and physically I could not feel anything, but whatever grabbed me was a real as the screams. I stopped before I took a single step. Then I turned, launched the canoe and paddled out to the center of the canal. I didn't have a choice.

The light grew. I don't mean it got brighter. It *grew*. By the time I got to the center of the canal, it was hovering a foot above the water like a malignant mist. I could feel it crawling over my skin, and I mean to tell you that it *wanted* me.

I leaned over and stared into the glowing water. Far below, maybe a hundred feet (and yes, when I floated over the same place the day before, it was maybe two or three feet deep), I saw a cave. The green light vomited out of its mouth, and there, within that light, human shadows moved. I gripped my paddle with the intent of getting back to land, but the instant I dug it into the water, something tugged at me, hard. I tried to fight it, but the canoe lurched and I was pulled overboard.

I screamed, I think. My vision blurred and then cleared. I was dragged to the bottom, toward the dancing shadows. The light pulled me into the cave. The rock walls closed in all around me. The screams grew louder, somehow not muffled at all through the water. I stared ahead, trying to see past the shadows. The cave narrowed, widened, and then narrowed again.

This is a dream, I told myself, and took great comfort in that fact. After all, there had been no

Barriers

sensation of drowning. That could only mean I was still in my canoe. Then my head bumped against an outcropping of rock. Neon stars shattered my vision and darkness closed in. I cried out in pain, and my voice gurgled. Water filled my lungs and I tried to expel it. Dream or not, it was far too real.

Suddenly the tunnel widened. I was pulled into a cavern perhaps the length and breadth of a football field. The ceiling and floor fell away, creating a vast open space. I found the source of the shadows. They were everywhere, crawling up the sides of the cavern, swinging pickaxes and shovels. There were hundreds of them, each one glowing with the same sick light that imprisoned me.

Here were the slaves who dug the canal, who labored in the oppressive heat, succumbing to disease and exhaustion. Death, it seemed, had not stopped them. They just changed directions and kept right on digging. Flesh that was both real and ethereal hung from their bones. Their faces were caved in husks. I could see fresh lash marks on the backs of those that still possessed a few shreds of skin. They dug and screamed, dug and screamed, dug and screamed.

I kept moving forward, toward the other end of the cavern. There, on a narrow ledge, stood the boss man, surveying his workers. He wore the garments of a wealthy man of a bygone era, although his clothes, and flesh, were just as tattered as those of his slaves. In his right hand he held a mean looking whip laced with bits of glass and metal. His back was to me as I drew near, but the instant my feet touched the ledge he turned to greet me.

It was John Gamble, of course. Here was the reason

the slaves continued to dig. I could see it in his sneer, in his glowing eye sockets, in his posture. We stared at each other, he the pre-civil war slaveowner, I his descendant, the twenty-first century scholar.

The earth shook. I whirled around in time to see the roof of the cavern give way. The slaves did not have a chance. They were swept off the walls and buried in an instant under tons of rock and dirt. Silt flew in every direction.

And still the screams continued. After a few minutes (or maybe several hours) the earth began to move. As I watched, the slaves dug themselves out. They emerged two and three at a time like worms squirming out of a rotten apple. Almost immediately they started digging again.

I turned back to Gamble, but now his face was gone. In its place was a pit of darkness. I stared into it and saw the end of light, the end of life itself. But it wasn't the darkness that filled me with loathing. There was something *in* the darkness, something ancient. It was something that lived in the depths of the earth, but not always.

In an instant, I was given knowledge that spanned all of time and space. I understood that I was staring at a creature that was old when humans were still swinging from trees. It was a creature that had roamed the stars like a god, confident in its own power. Sometime in a past so ancient as to be incomprehensible, it had met Another. They had fought. That battle had lasted eons and had nearly shattered reality itself. The creature had lost and fled, hiding from its terrible adversary. In time, it had found a place of life and light where it could hide, heal... and feed. John Gamble and his slaves were

Barriers

only a few of thousands, perhaps millions, of its prey.

I scrambled back, trying to get away. The green light winked out and I was left floating in darkness. Then something grabbed me. I could feel the water rush past my skin and I was certain that I was going to join the slaves in their eternal labor. My mind rebelled, and a darkness that had nothing to do with my surroundings flooded through me.

When I awoke, I was in the canoe, soaking wet. The sun was peeking through the trees in the west and night was on its way. For just a moment, I allowed myself to believe that it was over. Then the truth set in.

My skin was cold. There was no breath in my lungs, and when I moved, I could feel my body stiffening. I had no pulse.

I died in that underground cave. So why was I brought back? Perhaps it was a mercy, a few final hours in the light. Maybe, but I doubt it. When I looked into the pit that used to be John Gamble's face, I knew that I was staring at a creature that knew nothing of mercy or compassion. This was probably its idea of a final cruel joke.

The sun is nearly down. The mean green light is coming back, and soon it will transport me from the world of life where I no longer belong, and take me into the depths below. If I'm lucky, I'll join the slaves in their eternal digging, but I've got a terrible feeling that my fate will be far worse. The creature, I think, is finished with John. I think that it devoured his soul a little at a time, making it last for over a hundred and fifty years. Now it wants fresh meat and who better than one of John's descendants?

I've got to finish this journal. I'm going to wrap it in

my knapsack and throw it as hard as I can to the shore. Maybe somebody will find it. I just hope I have the dexterity and strength left to fling it. My arms and fingers are getting stiff.

I don't know why the creature chose this place. Perhaps it has its webs in many places, maybe even many times. I don't know why it forces the slaves to continue to dig, existing in a watery hell that they most certainly do not deserve. I just know that, right now, the light is growing, rising from the water. My time is gone.

Watch out for the sinkholes. Do you understand? The slaves keep digging, and every now and then, the earth caves in. That makes a sinkhole above. If it happens near you, get as far away as you can, because maybe, far below, John Gamble's slaves are digging, and screaming. Something else is there as well…something that does not belong in our world...something ravenous.

God help me.

One Piece at a Time

In the end, it was easy...gruesome, but easy. Dr. Aarav Chandra, Ph.D. M.SC., B.Sc, Sc.D. and certified genius, had chased the tail of time and space for over a decade as a theoretical physicist. Over the years he had held on to a steadfast belief that everything was quantifiable. The secrets of the universe could be unlocked with the key of pure mathematics. Now, at what was undoubtedly the end of a brilliant career, he could at least take some satisfaction in the fact that he had done it. He had figured it out, at least in part.

The irony of the situation was not lost on him. Eight years of college, another ten laboring in a lab at MIT, courtesy of a hefty government grant, and he had finally found the answer after a night of heavy drinking and a ridiculous movie.

The movie was *Somewhere in Time*. It starred a young, vital Christopher Reeve, long before he had been confined to a wheelchair. Aarav had squawked like a hyena in heat when his girlfriend Marcia had pulled it out of her purse, but she had reminded him firmly that it was her turn to pick. His own movie preferences ran along action and horror films, and he absolutely detested the genre known as the 'chick flick', but a few well placed pats and tugs from the persistent Marcia had quieted him down and they had watched the movie.

The premise was absurd. Reeve had been able to will himself into the past. There had been no flashing lights, no futuristic machinery, merely the actor lying in bed repeating over and over that it was a specific date in 1912. Aarav had groaned throughout the entire movie, irritating Marcia to the point that she left as soon as it was over. He had stumbled to the bathroom, assumed the age-old position on the toilet, and started thinking. He did not want to admit it, even to himself, but the more he thought about it, the more he wondered if there might be some deeper truth buried in the movie. Maybe ol' Chris was on to something, and if so, then maybe he was as well. Being extra careful not to jar this fragile, yet amazing, mental state, he went back to his living room.

Movement takes energy, he lectured himself over and over again, pacing through his apartment, sipping shot after shot of Jack Daniels whisky and slowly growing more and more inebriated. *Any kind of movement, including movement through time. That would take an obscene amount of energy. But…*

Maybe it was the perfect storm of alcohol, the movie and a genius level intellect, but slowly Aarav slid into a zone that few have ever been privileged to enter. Einstein had frequented it, along with Hawking, and most probably Kubrick. A handful of philosophers and writers had circled it from a distance. Most of humanity didn't even know it existed. It was a place where creativity and logic flowed equally…a place where time and space converged in the mind.

But…

There's an incredible amount of energy in the mind. Not electrical energy, but the energy of thought. Where does that energy go? Where do thoughts that have been thought go once they've been thought? The question made no sense, but he grabbed it by the tail and would not let it go. Without realizing it, he ambled back to the

Barriers

toilet and sat down. He began to visualize equations and his thought process slowly entered into a realm of pure mathematics. He could easily visualize the equations dancing in the air in front of him, slowly taking on greater and greater complexity.

Aarav was in the throws of an amazing creative effort. He was certain that, if he could find the right equations and put them in the right order, all he would have to do would be to speak them out loud and an entire cosmos would spring into being.

Then something happened. He rearranged part of an equation and, without any fuss, the flaw appeared. Spherical in shape and about the size of his fist, it was so black and featureless that it hurt his eyes just to look at it. It hung in the air over the bathtub to his right, exactly at eye level.

A memory surfaced through the glut of equations swirling through his mind. As a boy growing up in California, he had peered through a hole in his neighbor's fence...many times. On the other side there happened to be a pool and a teenage girl who liked bikinis. He understood that this sphere was in essence the same thing...a hole in the fence of space and time. He had not created it. He was certain of that. The flaw was a natural phenomenon, like a knot in a board or a bubble in a plane of glass. His foray into the Physics Zone, as he now thought of it, had merely made it visible.

He remained perfectly still. He feared that if he moved, he would jar the fragile ether on which his thoughts floated. He knew, without knowing how he knew, that if he slid out of the zone, he would never find his way back. It was only when something stirred in his peripheral vision that he dared turn his head. To his amazement, another flaw was hanging over the bathroom sink. Smaller than the first, it was in all other respects identical. He blinked, and in the space of that blink, the bathroom was suddenly filled with dozens of flaws in space and time, ranging in size from a golf ball to a beach ball. *That settles it,* he thought blearily. *There really is no God. The universe can't be this poorly constructed...*

Moving in slow motion, he turned to look at the original flaw. Alarm bells were screaming inside his head, but he did not care. He had to touch it. He *had* to. *One small stretch for man,* he lectured himself, and reached toward it. As he did, the flaw slowly moved away. He followed it with his hand, but whenever he came close, the flaw slid off to one side or another. It was as if it and his hand were magnets with opposing poles.

Hardly daring to breathe, Aarav got up. As he stood, the flaws skittered away. It took him almost two minutes to get to the bedroom. There were even more flaws in the hallway, and the bedroom itself was swimming with them. He glanced over toward the corner in time to see a particularly big one bounce across the top of his dresser. As it did so, it scooped up his car keys, swallowing them whole. Aarav tracked it to his nightstand where it landed again, this time depositing the keys next to his laptop. *I knew it,* he thought triumphantly. *I don't even want to look in my sock drawer.* His thought process quavered and he carefully pushed the revelation aside.

He moved over to the bed and lay flat on his back. The flaws continued their slow dance about the room.

Barriers

Each time one came close, it arced away, as if repelled by his organic nature. He was pretty sure that was it. He saw a pencil that was lying next to his keyboard disappear into a smaller flaw, only this time it did not return. Inanimate objects could pass through at will, it seemed.

He was suddenly consumed with a desire to thrust his head through one of those holes in the fence and see what was on the other side. The thought struck him that, if he could capture one, he could use it to unlock the mysteries that had baffled physicists since there had been physicists to baffle. He could come to grips with the true nature of the universe.

But how? he wondered hopelessly. *How can I touch something that was never meant to be touched?* In a mental state that was one part enlightened and three parts inebriated, he knew the answer. *I can't,* he moaned. *If I could, then so could someone else. We would have figured this out centuries ago.* The realization brought him up short. Others must have seen what he was seeing. He was good, perhaps the best in his field, but there were other gifted physicists as well. Why, then, were there no reports? *Simple,* he thought, answering his own question. *Probably the only way to see the flaws is to get blind, stinking drunk. I can see the equation now...a = 1/5 Jack Daniels, b = the time it takes to get stoned, and c = visualizing equations and numbers that simply can't exist in the physical universe. No problem. I'd better make room on my bookshelf for that Nobel Prize I'm going to get.* The thought struck him as funny and he started to giggle. Immediately his vision blurred and the flaws began to fade. A flash of panic brought him fully back into the zone and the

David F. Gray

flaws stabilized.

He breathed a sigh of relief, and without warning inspiration struck. He remembered something from one of the *Hitchhiker's Guide to the Galaxy* books by the late, great Douglas Adams. He was pretty sure it was from the fourth book in the trilogy, where the hero, Author Dent, learns how to fly. The answer was hilarious. Jump off a cliff or tall building and as you fall, forget to hit the ground. It was a good punchline, but in a heartbeat, it made prefect sense.

How do I become inorganic? he asked himself. *Simple. I forget that I am organic.* It was ridiculous of course, but for eighteen years he had trained his mind to think in very strict, very linear and very *un*-ridiculous lanes. Why not try a little absurdity?

Trying to reconstruct it later, he could never quite remember how he did it. He lay in his bed, much like Christopher Reeve had in a movie that now made perfect sense. Still flying high in the zone, and thinking exclusively in the language of mathematics, he worked through equation after equation. Suddenly a profound change washed over his innermost being. His heart still pumped blood, his brain still thought thoughts, but in a very real sense, he was different. It was as if he had pulled on a cloak that masked his true essence.

He opened his eyes and saw that several flaws were floating quite close. His heart rate doubled and he could feel his cloak quiver. He almost lost it, but managed to control himself. Shoving his excitement away, he slowly reached out to the nearest flaw. This time, it did not skitter away. This time it actually moved toward him. Knowing that the answers to all of time and space were waiting on the other side, he quelled a last-minute

Barriers

surge of fear and thrust his right hand into the flaw.

There was a slight tingling sensation, but no pain. As expected, his hand disappeared up to the wrist. What he did not expect was to see the flaw wink out, taking his hand with it. He jerked away, but his hand was gone. With an equal mixture of disbelief and horror, he stared at the cross section of his wrist. He could see everything quite clearly. Arteries, veins, pulsing blood, bone, it was all there, and somehow, so was his hand. He could feel it, as though it was still connected to his wrist. He wriggled invisible fingers, desperately trying to understand what was happening to him.

Fighting a rising panic, he started to wave his left hand over his stub of a wrist when another flaw swooped in and swallowed it whole. Aarav screamed and the entire roomed warbled. Other flaws were moving in, and now he was the one trying to skitter out of the way. His arms flailed and he could feel his hands track with them. They were somewhere else, and he understood that they were probably also some*when* else. Past? Future? In the kitchen? At his lab? In another universe? He had no idea. He flexed fingers that were out of sync with his own timeframe, trying to touch something familiar.

The flaws continued to close in. A rather large one took his left foot along with a respectable chunk of leg. Biting cold engulfed the missing member and he started to lose all feeling in it. Whimpering, he scrambled off the bed and tried to stand. He could feel his foot come with him, but it was no longer in his reality. He hopped a few steps on his remaining leg but then fell to the floor. Stifling a scream, he rolled over on his back. As if sensing wounded prey, the flaws swooped in. He tried to fight them off, but in a matter of seconds his arms were gone. A sphere the size of a basketball plunged through his abdomen, leaving a gaping hole. Two smaller ones took out his hips and three more plowed through his chest. His body started to resemble a slice of Swiss cheese.

Aarav was beyond horror now. Still in the zone, he understood that he was being flung across time and space, spread out over the cosmos in ever decreasing pieces. *Please,* he begged a deity that he did not believe in, *please let it be over soon.* Ignoring his plea, the flaws continued their grizzly work, until at last only Aarav's head was left. There was still no pain. With his left hand he could feel something hard and unyielding. In his right he gripped a large handful of sand. Part of his torso was under water, while another part was transmitting sensations he could not begin to describe.

Within seconds, it was over. The same basketball-sized flaw that had taken out his torso came back for seconds. Aarav could only watch as it fell from the ceiling, heading straight for his head. *Nononononono,* he begged, but it paid him no mind. It moved down to where he rested on the floor and then, without any fuss, ate his head.

Darkness swallowed him. There was no sensation of movement, but he felt as if he was traveling an unimaginable distance. The darkness was complete, and he knew that, if he had hands, he would not be able to see them even if he held them up before his eyes. His panic melted away and was replaced by a fatalistic sense of acceptance. He was starting to understand that he had not been dismembered, at least not in the strictest sense. He was still whole. His body simply

Barriers

existed in different places at different times.

The darkness changed. It did not lessen, but its very nature was altered. Aarav could feel the difference. His panic threatened to make an encore appearance but he pushed it aside. He had passed through a barrier, albeit one piece at a time, that few, if any, had ever passed through before.

Gradually he became aware of a tiny star of light hovering directly in front of him. Lacking any points of reference, he could not tell if it was inches or light years away. He only knew that it was there. As he watched, it slowly expanded until he was engulfed by a whiteness that was as complete and even as the darkness. *Heaven?* He discarded the idea, but would not have been at all surprised to hear a booming voice saying something like *I am the Lord* come at him from every direction. Having no other choice, he waited.

The transition came quickly this time. The whiteness faded, replaced by a setting that his mind refused to accept. Within seconds, he was standing (or rather, his head was hovering) in the living room of his apartment. *No way,* he thought. Could he have traveled in a massive loop? And what about the rest of him?

Before he had time to ponder these questions, he sensed a tingling in his left arm. He glanced down just in time to see it reappear, seemingly no worse for wear. As he watched, the rest of his body faded in, until at last he was whole again. He fell to his knees, sobbing in relief. Wherever he was, he was at least complete.

After several minutes, he was able to pull himself together (figuratively this time) enough to take an interest in his surroundings. It only took a cursory examination for him to realize that he had not come

David F. Gray

home. It was a close facsimile of his apartment, only there were no doors or windows. Both the main entrance and the hallway that led to his bathroom and bedroom were missing. The curtains covered only blank walls. In the far corner, where his television had been, was a replica of the desktop computer he kept in his bedroom. It sat facing the wall on a cheap looking stand. A rather uncomfortable looking office chair was placed in front of it. Feeling like David Bowman, he stepped over to the computer, but before he could turn the monitor on, there was a flash of light behind him, accompanied by a rush of air across his face. He swung around and saw that he had a visitor.

The man was old beyond ancient, clothed in a white robe that fell all the way to the floor. Once he might have been taller than Aarav's five feet nine inches, but time had bent his back to where he barely topped five feet. He leaned heavily on a thick wooden staff and regarded Aarav with obvious resignation. Aarav stumbled backward in surprise but then managed to steady himself. After losing himself all over time and space, meeting this creature was almost anticlimactic. Gathering his resolve, he stood up straight and opened his mouth. He was going to say something like 'My name is Aarav Chandra. I am a human from the planet Earth. I come in peace.' *Or pieces,* he thought, and stifled an urge to giggle.

The old man was having none of it. He held up a warning hand and Aarav got the message. He closed his mouth. His every movement reeking of unimaginable weariness, the old man shuffled over to the computer and motioned for Aarav to sit down in the chair. Swallowing a thousand questions, Aarav obeyed. As

Barriers

soon as he was down, the old man hit a key and the monitor disappeared, along with the entire wall in front of him. Aarav cried out in fear and recoiled. Before him hung what could only be the entire cosmos. His chair was perched just inches away from what his mind told him was a drop of infinite magnitude. The old man ignored his fear. He reached across Aarav's chest and grabbed the mouse. Aarav's mind barely had time to register the three-dimensional cursor that appeared hanging above the cosmos when the old man clicked the left button. Immediately the universe rushed at them. In a matter of seconds, he was staring at a single galaxy.

It's just a different kind of monitor, he thought, trying to reassure himself, but he already knew better. This was no simulation. He was looking at the real thing. Again, the old man clicked, and a part of the galaxy flew at him. Another click and he was staring at a blazing sun. 'Click' again and the sun rushed past him and there was the Earth, hanging above them in all its glory. Before he could digest the view, another click brought them over the North American continent. 'Click.' There was the eastern seaboard. 'Click' again, and there was his own city. Two more clicks and he was hovering above his own apartment complex, and one final click brought him into his living room.

"Wait…What…" He tried to frame a question, but again the old man silenced him with a sharp wave. With withered hands he tapped the F9 key, then the F3 key and finally the Enter key. For the final time, Aarav gasped. The living room was suddenly filled with the same flaws that had dismembered him and brought him here, only now, instead of dozens there were hundreds

...thousands.

Again, the old man moved the mouse. He placed the cursor over one of the flaws and with a right click, highlighted it. Then, making sure that he had Aarav's full attention, he hit the CRTL, ALT and DEL keys in rapid succession. As Aarav watched, the flaw slowly faded until it disappeared entirely. The old man highlighted another flaw and repeated the procedure, achieving the same results. He looked at Aarav expectantly. Aarav glanced up and for the first time met the old man's eyes.

During his senior year in high school, he had worked for Home Depot. His boss had been a fifty-something man who had spent over thirty years with the company, rising to the position of supervisor. Aarav could never forget his boss's tired eyes. They were the eyes of a man who had climbed as far as he would ever climb, and knew it. This withered old man clicking the mouse had the same eyes. With a sigh, he stood and nodded. It took Aarav a moment, but then he got it.

"Now just a darn minute," he snapped. He started to stand, but without any warning he was suddenly surrounded by three head-sized flaws. They hovered around him, waiting. Aarav immediately sensed a difference in these particular flaws and knew, without having to ask, that if one of them swallowed any part of his body, that part would not be coming back. These flaws were a one-way trip, and they were *hungry*. He held up his hands and *slowly* sat down. The old man stared at him, waiting. Turning, Aarav repeated the old man's procedure. He picked out a flaw and made it go away.

The old man nodded in weary satisfaction. Reaching

under the computer stand, he pulled out a book about the size and thickness of a phone book. Glancing down, Aarav saw that there were at least another dozen books stacked up next to his feet. The old man plopped the book down next to the keyboard and flipped it open to the first page. Aarav recognized the diagram, a floor plan to his own apartment, immediately. The old man pointed to the diagram, and then turned the page. Another floor plan, probably the apartment next to his, was laid out. Another flip and another floor plan presented itself. Heart sinking, Aarav got it. These diagrams were his work orders.

Satisfied, the old man turned and walked away. This time there was no flash of light. The old man merely faded as he left. After four steps he was gone. The hungry flaws stayed behind for a few moments, but then they faded as well. Aarav was not fooled. If he tried to escape, they would reappear. A cold realization was settling over him. He had been shanghaied...conscripted as cheap labor...or more accurately, slave labor; his task - to repair the universe, one square foot at a time.

Suppressing a shudder and knowing that the killer flaws were just out of sight, he highlighted another flaw and erased it. Were there others like him? Was it possible to find them, or at least communicate with them? He doubted it. He was almost certainly separated from them by greater barriers than the walls of his bogus apartment.

Point. Click. CTRL – ALT –DEL. He went about his task, his mind working furiously to figure a way out of his predicament.

Point. Click. CTRL – ALT – DEL. Could he use the

David F. Gray

flaws again, this time to get out of here? Doubtful. Not counting the three the old man had called forth, this was almost certainly a flaw-free zone.

Point. Click. CTRL – ALT –DEL. How did the old man get in and out? Given enough time, maybe he could figure it out.

Aarav continued to work, eliminating flaw after flaw, but the number hovering in his living room did not seem to diminish. Was there a quitting time? What about lunch, and other breaks? He doubted that there was any kind of worker's union to protect him from what were probably very long hours.

Point. Click. CTRL –ALT – DEL. He *had* to find a way home. He was a genius, for crying out loud. He had multiple degrees. He was not about to spend the rest of his life working as a glorified office assistant/repairman. Point. Click. CTRL – ALT – DEL. He thought of Marcia, and suddenly wanted nothing more than to go home and apologize for making fun of her movie. He vowed silently to do exactly that, the instant he escaped. Point. Click. CTRL – ALT – DEL.

Maybe there were other doorways besides the flaws. Maybe this computer, which was obviously so much more than a simple desktop, held his answers. And if all else failed, he would somehow find other flaws, and use them. Anything, even the idea of being spread out across the cosmos, was better than spending the rest of his days here in this sterile cubicle. He would find his way home, even if he had to do it one piece at a time.

Barriers

The Call of Cats on a Pale Moon Night

The baby cried, dragging Charlie out of the first real night's sleep he had managed in over a month. *God, I really hate cats,* he thought, rolling over on his stomach. The king-sized bed squeaked in protest. He had meant to replace the mattress months ago, when it still mattered. Now, he couldn't care less. Reaching up, he pulled down a single blade of the blinds that covered the window at the head of his bed. He tried to ignore the empty space beside him, but since it was a perfect match for the empty space in his heart, he failed miserably. With bleary eyes he peered through the window, trying to locate the source of the eerie cry.

His lower middle-class neighborhood was shrouded in midnight darkness, although the full moon above cast harsh, silver wedges over the nearby houses. He knew all of them well, had seen most of the built, in fact. He could still remember Sulphur Springs as it had been almost forty years ago, when he and Lucille had moved in to what would become their only home. Then, most of the surrounding area had been empty fields and orange groves. Now, houses of all shapes and sizes, most of them well into the later stages of decay, crowded together in no discernable pattern. For over four decades, property values had plummeted, along with the ethics of far too many residents.

Another cry sounded through the closed window, and Charlie suppressed a shudder. The sound was all too human. He could easily believe that some lonely and frightened mother had abandoned her infant child beneath the shrubs under his window. He knew better, of course. Gangs of cats prowled the neighborhood at will.

He heard the blinds rustle and realized that his hand was trembling. The Parkinson's was getting worse, and the drugs were becoming less and less effective. Sooner or later, his brain would start to scramble the messages it was sending to his heart and lungs and that would be that. It really did not bother him too much. If there was some kind of afterlife, then Lucille was on the other side, waiting for him. If not...well, he really did not want to go through eternity without her anyway.

The cry came again, only this time it was accompanied by rage filled hissing. *Cat fight,* he thought. *Somebody peed in somebody's turf.* The hissing continued for another thirty seconds and then shut off. Charlie waited, counting his heartbeats, but it seemed that the skirmish was over. With a heavy sigh, he closed his eyes and, after several minutes, drifted back into an uneasy sleep.

The screech came from right under his window, and he jerked awake, his heart pounding. *Give a guy a break,* he pleaded to the cats, God and whoever else might be listening. He grabbed a fistful of blinds and yanked them down. Pressing his forehead against the glass, he saw three small, lithe shapes dart away, disappearing into the darkness across the street. He closed his eyes and two large tears rolled down his cheeks. He hated cats almost as much as he hated his empty bed...almost as much as he hated that drunken fool in the BMW who had ended Lucille's life. *Just go away,* he begged. *Just go away and let me die in peace.*

Maybe they heard him. Several minutes dragged until, gradually, the demands of his aging body took

Barriers

over. His breathing slowed and his thoughts grew muddy and indistinct. In a half-dream, he ran through the neighborhood, searching for something. It was close, so close that he could taste it. If he could find it, then his pain would end. He would have peace. He pressed deeper and deeper into the deserted streets until...

The growl was low this time, low and dangerous. Charlie opened his eyes and discovered that he had fallen asleep against the windowsill. His hand was numb from the weight of his forehead. With a sense of hopelessness, he looked thorough the blinds and saw what he knew he would see.

Four distinct, dark shapes dotted his front yard. They formed a rough square and all of them were facing in toward each other. He could not shake the impression that they were communing on a level that no human could ever hope to understand. The drowsiness dropped away from his mind as he studied the felines. *What do you talk about?* he thought. *What are you hiding? Where do you go?* As soon as that last question passed through his mind, Charlie swallowed hard. He was suddenly afraid.

"Where do you go?" he whispered aloud. The instant he spoke, the largest cat turned and dashed toward him. Before he could even cry out, it leaped onto the windowsill and hunkered down. Its green eyes glowed softly in the darkness, and even through the glass Charlie could hear the low rumble coming from deep within its chest. He wanted to pull away from the window and go back to sleep, but he was held in place by something that he could not begin to understand. The cat's eyes bored into his. With a thrill of fear, he realized that they really were glowing. It was not a trick of the light. Charlie felt his mouth go dry and his heart rate triple. He could feel the presence of the cat, but more that that, he could feel the will of the animal as it pressed against his own mind.

Where do you go? The question flittered through his mind again.

Come and see. Come and see. He did not hear the words, he felt them. The big cat jumped down and rejoined his companions. Now all four cats were staring at him. He could hear their call. *Come and see. Come and see.*

He pulled away from the blinds and sank back into his bed. His hand reached out for his mate of over forty years. *She's there,* he thought, desperately willing it to be true. *She's right there. I know it. I believe it, and all I have to do is reach a little further and I can touch her. I can. I can. I can.* His hand met only empty space.

Come and see. Come and see. The three words echoed through his mind and through his heart. He knew that he had to obey. He had to go and see.

He did not remember getting out of bed or getting dressed. He found himself at his front door, his hand on the knob. He hesitated, and for a single moment, he was free to choose. The growing fear in his heart was screaming at him to turn around and go back to bed. *There are worse things than grief,* he thought. *And there are things worse than death. Come on, Charlie. Let's go back to bed where we belong.*

He almost made it.

He stepped back from the door and turned to look at the living room. It was neat, well ordered, and above all, empty...as empty as the bedroom. His children were

Barriers

gone and his wife was dead.

There was nothing for him here.

He opened the door and stepped out into the night.

The cats were waiting. *Come and see.* The single thought wafted through his mind like the faintest of summer breezes, but the call bound him with ties stronger than iron.

As he drew near, the cats took off. He followed them down the street, away from his house, never once looking back. Above, the moon shone with a brilliance he had never seen before. When he got to the end of the street, he could no longer recognize his own neighborhood. It was shrouded in darkness, and things once familiar were now strange and grotesque. *I'm entering their world,* he thought. *They move about in my world, but this is where they really live.* He glanced up at the blazing moon, feeling its beams of light caressing his face. *And you're the gatekeeper.* He did not understand, but understanding was not required.

On and on they led him, through twisted back streets that both did and did not exist. They passed through darkened yards that held things that had once been familiar. Swing sets, picnic tables, sandboxes, he knew what they were, but he no longer knew what they meant. Every so often he would glance at his escort, and each time he did, he saw that it had increased in size. Four became eight, and eight became sixteen.

The moonlight led the way. It opened strange doors, penetrating barriers he never knew existed. It led him deeper into this dark, unseen world. With every step, he could feel his past life slipping away. His mind was a hurricane of fear, but he could not resist the will of the small creatures that surrounded him. He kept moving.

David F. Gray

At length, he stepped into a large vacant lot. A high fence surrounded it on all sides, and only a small gate opened in from the street. As he entered, he saw bed frames and car parts and washing machines scattered about. There were rusting lawnmowers and frames of bicycles and a hundred other shapes that he once may have recognized. The cats ran past him, disappearing and reappearing through countless hidden nooks and crannies. As if in a dream, Charlie crept to the center of the lot. Something was there, he knew. Something was waiting for him. He slipped around a rusting water heater and saw her.

Mother, he thought, and indeed she was. The cat was huge, at least the size of a panther. Her fur was a mottled gray, and her eyes were blazing with a pure white radiance, the same radiance generated by the moon. She was lying in a hole that had been dug out by the paws of her willing servants. She was ready to give birth. *Come and see,* echoed the command through his mind.

"I can see," he whispered.

A sharp, biting pain lanced through his right ankle. Looking down, he saw that two of his former escorts were gnawing at his sock. He gasped in pain and tried to pull away, but his body would not obey the commands of his mind. Mother held him in her will, and he could not defy her. Two more cats moved to his other ankle. Teeth and claws tore into the barely protected flesh, sending waves of searing agony through his body. He tried to scream, but his jaws clenched together, bent to the will of a lifeforce far greater than his own. More cats joined in, their teeth ripping through flesh and muscle and finally, bone.

Barriers

For an instant, Charlie's mind broke free of Mother, although his body was still held immobile. One final moment of lucidity was granted him, and a weak moan of pure despair slipped through his lips. He wanted to go home. He wanted to go back and die a peaceful death. He wanted to see what wonders lay beyond the veil of this life. He wanted to find Lucille again.

As his body was systematically ripped apart, he understood what was happening. It was all being stripped away. What he might have become after his death, what higher levels of being he could have ascended to, Mother was stealing all of it.

His left ankle gave way and he fell backward. His head hit something hard as he landed and he felt the breath burst from his lungs. The remaining cats swarmed over him, chewing and devouring. Three of them found his exposed throat and went to work. He felt his windpipe give way. Soon after his carotid artery was opened. Blood spurted upward in an obscene fountain, and mercifully Charlie's world began to fade. His eyes found the impossibly bright moon and fastened on it. As everything else dimmed, it became the only object in his universe. Then, when all else was gone, it too winked out.

He became aware of crushing warmth. He could not breathe and he began to struggle. He had to get out. Panic set in. He knew that if he did not break free soon, he would die. He thrashed about, pushing forward. Then, when he was sure that he would suffocate, he found open air. His lungs screamed in agony. With one final push, he forced his way free of the warmth. The air tingled over his wet fur, and his eyes opened for the first time. The first thing he saw was the moon, and he knew that it would be a constant companion all the days of his life.

He struggled feebly, his strength nonexistent. He needed food. He could sense blood nearby, and it awakened a hunger within his innermost being. *Not yet,* said something deep within his mind. *Soon, but not now.* What he needed was even closer. Squirming past his newborn brothers and sisters, he found one of Mother's teats and began to suck.

A very distant part of him, the part that had once been a man, screamed in agony. He had been close to the end of his life, and would soon have tasted of the mysteries beyond death. Now that was stripped from him forever. He had lost eternity and had become...something else.

Far across an abyss that only a human could travel, another being cried out in pure grief, for a mate had been forever lost.

As Mother's milk flowed into him, his senses began to awaken, and remnants of the man faded. His soul was bound to this form, and the former things were passing away. His old life was now nothing more than a shadow.

Exhausted from his birth, and sated with Mother's milk, the newborn kitten snuggled into the warmth of Mother's body. In time, he would explore this strange new realm. He would defend his territory against other tribes. He would run with his brothers and mate with his sisters. He would live in the silver shadows cast by the ever-present moon. Above all, he would bend himself to Mother's will. He was one of her countless brood, now, and would serve her all the days of his life.

As he drifted into a deep sleep, the remaining shreds

of his humanity dissolved into nothingness. The man that was slipped into oblivion and the kitten dreamed of the battles and blood to come.

He was content.

David F. Gray

The Bridge

A Manuscript Found In A Diner

I traveled through a barren land until, at daybreak of a certain day, I crested a steep rise and came to the City by the River. The morning sun struck the glass walls of the many tall, majestic buildings, refracting into a blazing array of colors that dazzled my eyes. I was tempted to remain in that city, for it was beautiful, but it was not my final destination.

Beyond the shining City was the River, although 'ocean' would be a more apt description. The distant shore was invisible. The churning waters swirled with treacherous currents. Endless waves crashed against the city's levies in a constant struggle to breach the concrete walls and engulf the fragile glass buildings.

The only way across the River was the Bridge.

Who had built it and how it had been built, these things were lost to time. It was a hulking, multi-leveled beast. Its massive gray steel girders crisscrossed in mystifying patterns, jutting over a thousand feet into the air. The great pylons that supported it plunged into the dark waters of the River, driving deep into the earth. Far in the distance, I could see a distinct hump; a sloping metal mountain near what I assumed to be the Bridge's center. It brought to my mind the image of a giant boa constrictor in the process of digesting its latest meal.

There were two levels specifically for motor vehicles, both with eight well marked lanes. Above them, the top level was reserved strictly for pedestrians.

Barriers

It was lined with numerous shops and stalls provided by the enterprising citizens of the city, offering the traveler food, clothing and various diversions.

It was said that the land beyond the Bridge was a beautiful green country where people from all walks of life lived in peace and prosperity. For that reason, traffic only ran in one direction. No one who crossed the Bridge ever returned. I had searched long and hard for that land, and now that my feet were finally on the right path, I was determined to make the crossing as soon as possible.

I entered the City and found the people friendly enough. There were winding brick streets and lush, neatly manicured parks with sparkling fountains. I threaded my way through these streets until I finally came to a wide pedestrian thoroughfare that led to the River. From there I followed a sparse crowd to a steep ramp. Then, after an eternity of wandering, I climbed the ramp, crossed the threshold and stepped onto the Bridge.

The massive gray girders rose up on either side, joined by countless crossbeams high above. Their sheer size made me feel small and insignificant, and I unconsciously hunched my shoulders as I moved onto the wide pedestrian thoroughfare. The vendors in the stalls hawked their goods. They shouted at me as I went past, but I ignored them. I had enough food in my backpack to last at least a week. Water was not a concern. Cisterns had been spaced evenly along the pedestrian level, although I did not relish the idea of drinking the dark water of the River.

The concrete surface of the upper level vibrated as countless vehicles trundled along the lower levels, and high overhead the girders sang a mournful song as the wind whipped through them. As I moved forward, I suddenly felt dizzy. It was as if the Bridge was wobbling, about to come crashing down upon me. It took a while, but I finally acclimated to the noise and the vibration and picked up my pace.

After a while, curiosity got the better of me. I eased over to the right side of the Bridge, wanting to get a look at the River. There was no guardrail or any kind of fence. The girders rising up from below were several feet thick. Between them, about every twenty feet or so, was nothing but empty space. The pavement simply ended in a sharp edge that led to the churning water far below.

I grabbed onto the edge of a girder and leaned forward, but in that instant the vibrations seemed to increase. My strength left me and I sank to my knees. It occurred to me that all I had to do was lean forward. I would fall off the Bridge and smash into the River, my broken body sinking into oblivion. Suddenly I cried out as if awakening from some terrible nightmare. I could feel the water calling to me. I fell backward onto the pavement and scrambled away from the edge.

"Best not do that again." I swallowed and took a deep breath, trying to calm my pounding heart as I sought the source of that admonition. My first impression was teeth...straight and white. The thin lips that normally covered them were pulled open in a wide grin. I nodded at the teeth, giving myself an extra second to take in the rest of the face.

It belonged to a youngish man, as did the body that was connected to it. His head was covered with an unruly shock of blond hair that I found somehow

Barriers

unsettling. He wore a simple white polo shirt and jeans. A pair of round, rimless glasses were perched high on his forehead, half covered by his hair. He leaned on the counter of what I assumed was his shop just a few feet away, regarding me with glittering brown eyes.

"Agreed," I managed to say. "I don't know what came over me."

"It's the water," said the man. "If it calls to you, best stay away from the edge."

"No problem," I muttered, scrambling to my feet.

"May I offer you something from my shop?" said the man. I glanced behind him and saw that his 'shop' was a simple wooden stall that had been stocked with such goods as bottled water and assorted snacks.

"Thanks," I replied, "but I'm fine."

"You'll need water," said the man. "Mine is imported directly from the City." I didn't like the look of him, but after my experience at the edge, I was doubly certain that I did not want to drink from the cisterns. I had a large canteen that I wore around my waist, but that was the extent of my water supply.

"I'll take some water," I said. He grinned again and pulled four bottles off his shelf. I paid quickly and stuffed them into my backpack.

"Be sure to sleep lightly," said the man. "There are things here that dwell in the lower levels. Sometimes they come up, looking for something to eat." He saw the look of sudden fear on my face and snickered. Embarrassed, I threw him a parting scowl, adjusted my pack and stormed away.

The rest of the day was uneventful and I made good time. As daylight faded, I looked for a place to sleep. There were no inns or hostels. I found a space between two large shops that was secluded enough for my needs. I made myself as comfortable as possible, ate a light meal and then, lulled by the steady thrum of the lower levels, drifted into a deep, dreamless sleep.

* * *

And so began my journey across the Bridge. As the days went by, the atmosphere on the upper level gradually became more like a carnival. There were barkers promising wonders beyond imagination behind their brightly colored curtains. Wandering groups would break into song and dance whenever the mood took them, eagerly scooping up the coins appreciative travelers would toss their way. Food was plentiful and cheap, and most of the booths offered water as well.

Maybe a week into my journey, at about mid-day, I chanced upon a solitary stairwell perched on the left side of the Bridge. From the outside it looked as if an elevator had simply risen to the top level while leaving its shaft behind. It seemed so out of place that I felt compelled to investigate.

I approached the door to the stairwell as if it were a portal to some strange and dangerous land. The door was made of steel, and the surrounding shell solid concrete. I peered through a wire laced rectangular window and saw plain, concrete stairs leading down. There was no handle, so I gave the door an experimental shove. To my surprise it opened easily. I glanced over my shoulder to see if anyone might be coming to stop me, but no one was even looking in my direction. With a 'what the hell' shrug I stepped into the stairwell. The door closed behind me with a loud click.

Barriers

Feeling adventurous I started down.

The stairwell smelled musty, as if it had not been used for a very long time. The plain concrete steps were unstained, and there were no scratches on the painted yellow handrail. I moved slowly, half expecting to encounter some sort of security guard, but no one stopped me.

The stairwell was divided into segments of ten steps each, zigzagging downward. The sounds of the lower levels grew louder as I descended. By the time I reached the door that led to the next level, six segments later, my ears were ringing. There was no window in this door, but like the one above it was not locked. I eased it open and stuck my head through the narrow crack.

And just as quickly I pulled back, slamming the door shut behind me. I slumped against it, trembling. The door opened onto a narrow sidewalk, no more than two feet wide. Beyond that was the main thoroughfare, all eight lanes of it. Cars, trucks, mobile homes and every other vehicle imaginable went zooming along the lanes, whipping past the door with speeds that should have been impossible. Bumper to bumper, they whizzed by me so close that if I had leaned any further, my head would have been bludgeoned into a wet, pulpy mess. I almost returned to the upper level. By my estimation, I had at least another two weeks of travel ahead of me, but something seemed to draw me downward. I grabbed the handrail and resumed my descent.

The door on the next level was identical to the first, but this time I was a great deal more cautious. I placed my ear against the cold metal surface but could hear nothing beyond. Slowly I opened it, peeking through

David F. Gray

the narrow crack. This time I did not draw back in terror. This time I simply stared.

Like the level above, there were eight lanes spanning the width of the Bridge, but instead of countless vehicles racing along at insane speeds, this level was deserted. I opened the door wide enough to slide out, pressing against the concrete wall, but my precautions were needless. The lower level was empty. I stepped away from the door.

Across the lanes I could see the dull red sun glaring through the girders. I glanced behind me and saw that the stairwell was the only solid surface along the closer edge. On either side, the gun metal gray girders reached up to the upper levels and down to...what? Puzzled, and more than a little afraid, I edged back to the door and slid into the stairwell. Once again I almost returned to the upper level, but my curiosity was now running in high gear. Was there another level? I had to know.

The traffic sounds faded as I continued my descent. By the time I reached the bottom of the staircase, they had dissipated entirely. I stood there, staring at the final door. Unlike the others, it was pitted and rusted. The single light set into the ceiling was dim and yellow.

I pressed my hand against the surface of the door, pulled it away and saw that my palm was black with soot. I grabbed the handle with both hands and pulled. It did not budge. I set my feet against the concrete floor and heaved, but with no success.

I nearly gave up, but with a grunt I gave the door one final pull and was rewarded with a loud, harsh scrape. Startled, I pulled away. That noise had sounded less like metal against concrete and more like the scream of some damned soul. I hesitated. Then, with a final burst of determination, I pulled with all my strength. The scraping grew even louder as the door slowly opened. After several seconds I finally made an opening wide enough to squeeze through. I stuck my head through the crack and drew in a sharp breath.

This final level was a parking lot. Cars and trucks, both old and new, were sitting in the lanes, neatly placed in near perfect lines as if waiting to roll in a parade of some kind. Fascinated, I stepped off the sidewalk and threaded my way through the narrow spaces between the cars. There was no sign of disaster, natural or otherwise. It looked as if the owners had simply parked them and walked away.

I could hear the sound of waves breaking against the girders. Drawn by the sound, I edged past the rows of cars until I reached the far edge of the Bridge. Like the levels above, there was no guardrail, but unlike them, there was no real danger in dying from a fall. The water was barely a foot below where I stood.

I looked out across the River, regarding the dark, choppy water with a growing sense of unease. I could feel the unimaginable weight of the Bridge above me. I decided that enough was enough. I turned and started toward the stairwell, determined to resume my crossing. I was desperate to find peace in that far green country.

As I threaded my way through the deserted cars, I caught a glint of light to my right. I looked and saw a small, flickering flame a few dozen yards away. The idea of a fire around so many cars was unsettling. If one were to catch alight it would probably explode. As close as they were to one another, that could start a chain reaction that might weaken the Bridge.

My first impulse was to get back to the upper level and get moving, but the more I thought about a massive explosion on this lowest level, the more frightened I became. Could the Bridge, as strong as it was, withstand the force of all those cars exploding? I'm not a hero. In fact, I am rather selfish, usually acting in my own best interests. It was that selfishness that motivated me to turn toward the fire and investigate. I did not want to die on the Bridge.

The cars were parked so close together that I had to squeeze between them. The fire grew closer, and as it did I saw that it was actually a contained bonfire. A clearing of sorts had somehow been created between the cars. It was rectangular space about thirty feet wide and spanning all eight lanes. The bonfire was burning in a large barrel in the center of the clearing. Huddling around it, in a rough circle, stood a few dozen people. Some were talking, some were merely staring into the fire. The group seemed harmless enough. Curious, I stepped forward. A grizzled old man saw me.

"You are welcome here," he said in a surprisingly deep voice. He was bald, his wrinkled scalp covered with brown age spots, but his blue eyes were bright and alert. "Come and warm yourself by our fire." In my entire time on the Bridge I could not recall feeling hot or cold, but the instant he spoke to me I shuddered with a sudden chill. I stepped into the circle with a nod of gratitude and held my hands toward the fire, embracing its warmth. As I did, I studied my new companions.

They were a diverse group, ranging in age from young adult to the very old. Racially they were mixed as well, with skin tone going from pale white to deep brown. About a third of the group was female. All of

Barriers

them were dressed casually, most in jeans or worn work clothes. My first thought was that they were some kind of loose association of beggars, but none of them looked malnourished. There was also an odd sense of familiarity about them, particularly the old man.

"You are persistent. I'll give you that much," said the old man. I jumped a little. I had not heard him come up beside me. I collected myself and turned to face him.

"Excuse me?"

"How long for you?" he said, answering my question with a question.

"You mean on the Bridge?" I asked, and he nodded. "A week...I think," I said. Suddenly I wasn't so sure. Had it truly been a week? It felt much longer. The old man nodded and smiled, but his eyes were troubled and sad.

"You know that this is not true," he said softly. I edged away from him, not caring for the turn the conversation was taking.

"Granted I may have lost a day or two," I said. "They do tend to run together here."

"Some make the crossing quickly," said the old man. "They are carried by their gods in swift chariots of iron and steel." He glanced up and I understood he was talking about the second level. "Others make their way on foot. Their journey is longer but no less valid." He looked at me again. "Still others lose their way during the crossing. They wait here until they gather the strength to go on." He reached out and tapped me on the chest.

"And then there are those like you," he said. "You don't belong on any level, even that which is closed until the end of days, and yet you continue to try. How many times must we meet like this? Each time I hope that you will manage to retain some scrap of memory from before, and each time I am disappointed." My discomfort transmuted into full blown fear.

"I think that it's time for me to go," I said.

"What did you do before you came to the Bridge?" said the old man. The circle of people closed behind me. I was certain that I was going to be murdered and tossed into the River.

"Please don't hurt me," I said...begged, actually.

"You are in no danger, and may leave as soon as you answer my question," said the old man. "What did you do before you came to the Bridge?" I tried to back away but bumped into one of the younger men, who gently pushed me forward.

"I...I...wandered," I said.

"Where?" demanded the old man.

"In...a barren place," I said. I tried to pin down the memories of my travels, but my mind refused to focus. I could remember nothing but the barren land.

"And before that?" said the old man.

"I...I..."

"You don't remember," said the old man.

"Please let me go."

"Not until you remember," said the old man. "Too many times you have come here, and too many times you have left, only to forget everything and repeat the cycle." I pushed away again, only to be shoved back toward the center.

"Where...were...you?" The old man's words struck like the blows of a hammer, driving deep into my mind, and as they did, I remembered.

"I died," I said, and the simple truth in those two

small words cut me to my core.

"How?" said the old man. I shook my head. "HOW?"

"I DON'T KNOW," I shouted. The old man held my gaze a moment longer and then his shoulders slumped.

"Of course you don't," he said. He waved at the circle. "You are free to go. I have no doubt that we will meet again."

"Why?" I whispered. The old man shook his head.

"I don't know," he said. "You refuse to remember. Until you do, you will remain as you are. I am truly sorry." He waved me away. "You need to go now. I wish you peace, but I am afraid that you will never find it." The crowd moved aside. I wanted to stay and find answers, but the old man's face was unyielding. I edged through the broken circle and with a last, longing glance at the fire, made my way back to the stairwell.

* * *

I will tell what little there is left to tell before it is gone from my mind completely. By the time I reached the upper level I was famished. I wondered at this. Why does a dead man need to eat? I found a quiet corner, dipped into my pack, and ate a hearty meal. As I did, I studied my fellow pedestrians carefully. Now that I knew the truth, I understood that I was witnessing the procession of the dead to the next life. More than witnessing, I was a part of it.

No one looked dead. They were of every race; men, women and children, some laughing and talking, some simply walking, their eyes and minds focused on their destination. I began to understand a marvelous truth.

David F. Gray

Death is but a transition from one life to the next. The Bridge was a real, solid thing in a real, solid world, but it was also far more than that. It was a path that led from the world behind me to the world ahead. These worlds were also real. Suddenly I was filled with immeasurable joy. Death, that dread thing that all mortals fear and yet must endure, was behind me. Before me was a land of peace and plenty. I finished my meal, shouldered my pack and resumed my journey.

Several days passed. The hump in the center of the Bridge grew closer. As it did, my joy faded. It soared above me, the grade steep and daunting. The maze of girders overhead soared with it, following its contour. I could see my fellow pilgrims ascending. They seemed to have no trouble, but as I drew near, the thought of crossing that artificial mountain of steel and concrete filled me with dread.

How shall I describe that climb? Even now my hands tremble as I record that final leg of my journey. I started up the hump, leaning forward, and immediately a strong wave of vertigo smashed into me. I almost turned around, but some sense of desperation kept me going. Each step was a small victory, but with each step the grade seemed to increase. The crest of the hump did not seem to draw any closer. I could feel my fellow pilgrims around me, but I also felt as if I was now alone on the Bridge.

Once, at about the halfway mark, I glanced over my shoulder, trying to judge how far I had come. I screamed, for I felt as if I was clinging to the face of a sheer cliff with the base of the hump thousands of feet below. My world spun madly for a moment and I nearly fell backward. I knew that if I did, I would

Barriers

plummet to...what...my death? Oblivion? Instead, I fell forward, arms outstretched, landing on the hard pavement.

I crawled from then on, inch by inch, keeping my eyes on the concrete directly beneath my eyes. The wind began to blow, hitting me head on. I had to close my eyes against the grit and gravel hurled into my face.

I reached the top, and when I did, I wept. Inches from where I stopped, the Bridge ended. It was as if some great force had simply chopped off a wide section, leaving nothing but a sheer drop into the River far below. In the distance, I could see where the Bridge continued, sloping downward in a gentle grade and continuing on to the land beyond. I could just get a glimpse of that land. It was beyond beautiful. It was paradise. It was *home*. And it was denied to me. There was no way to cross that great empty space.

I don't know how long I clung to the edge, but eventually it came to my mind that I should go back to that old man and join his circle of friends by the fire. *They wait here until they gather the strength to go on*, he had said. That then, was my hope. I would wait with the others until I could figure out how to move on. And I *would* figure it out.

I gathered my resolve and began to crawl away from the gulf, but the instant I moved, the wind hit me with massive force. Now, though, it was coming from behind, pushing me forward. I grabbed at the pavement, but there was no purchase. I was forced to the edge, and then forced over the edge. Screaming, I fell, and as I fell, I remembered.

I had a life...a good life. There was a beautiful woman who loved me, children who adored me, and a profession that had been very good to me. In what seemed like an instant, it had all been ripped away. There had been a scandal (my fault), and a cancer growing in my wife (not my fault). My profession was lost, and the respect I had spent years cultivating was destroyed. My children disowned me and the one person who stood by me through the entire mess was dying.

One morning I drove her to her doctor's appointment for the chemotherapy that was nearly as bad as the cancer. I left her there with the promise to return. Instead, I drove to one of the bridges that crossed the wide river near the hospital. I stopped at the center, got out of my car, and with barely a moment's hesitation, jumped. I remembered falling, and I remembered hitting the water.

After that, there was the never-ending cycle of the Bridge.

How many times had I tried to make the crossing, only to be denied? How many more times would I try? How long must I endure this punishment? There were no answers, of course. I slammed into dark water that was as hard and unyielding as the steel of the Bridge. I felt every bone in my body shatter. I sank into the freezing darkness, praying to I don't know who for the mercy of oblivion.

I started to dissolve. My arms, my legs, and finally my torso, all faded as the black water obliterated them. My head went last, and yet, even when it was gone, I continued to sink, awake and aware. *This has to be hell.* It was my last coherent thought. The pressure of the water increased, and as it did I could feel my mind, or soul, or spirit, or whatever I had become start to

Barriers

compact. I was squeezed into a tiny, fading spark. That spark grew smaller and smaller, until, at last, darkness took me.

And then...

I found myself once more in a barren land. I remembered everything; my old life, my previous attempts to cross the Bridge, the gulf that denied me access to paradise...everything. But the memories were fading fast. I had to do something to stop the cycle, so I found a small diner. Now, sitting in a booth next to a window that overlooks the road to the Bridge, I am writing it all down. I have to hurry. Even now I look back at the first few pages and it is as if they have been written by a stranger.

I have to believe that someday, I will be allowed to make the crossing. I know I did a terrible thing, but others have done far worse. I'm not a murderer, or a rapist, or a thief. All I did was reach the point where I could not go on. Maybe I abandoned my wife when she needed me the most, but it's not like I killed her...is it?

Perhaps that is my punishment. Perhaps I will not be able to make the crossing until I find her on this side. If she forgives me, then maybe we can make the crossing together. Until then, I will keep trying. I will keep these pages with me and use them as a guide. When I come to the Bridge, I will know to stop and stay with the old man until somehow, I am able to find my wife. Then, together, we will find our way home.

* * *

Well boss, he did it again. Walked right through the front door and begged for a pen and some paper. If

David F. Gray

you ask me (and you never do), it's creepy how he manages to write the same story, word for word, each and every time. As soon as he was done, he left. Of course, he forgot his manuscript. I nearly ran after him, but you said that it wouldn't matter.

I know we're here to help these folk along on their journey, and I know for some that journey lasts a very long time, but I really feel for this poor bastard. Sure, he did a bad thing, but the idea of being trapped like that... well, as far as I'm concerned, he doesn't deserve that kind of punishment.

Anyway, here's his latest manuscript. I don't know why you bother to read it, since it's always the same, but I guess it doesn't matter one way or the other. He'll be back soon enough.

Barriers

Wade Flick

I rapped on the shaky wooden door three times. Long seconds passed while I stood there, sweating in the Florida heat. Finally, Wade Flick opened the door and frowned. He was not pleased to see me. He never is. When I contact him, I'm either out of time or out of options. On this particular night I happened to be out of both.

He was expecting me, of course. I always call ahead. Common courtesy aside, I owe him a lot. It's hard enough being a cop in this day and age and a good detective is always looking for an edge. Wade was my edge.

It was almost midnight when he let me in to his small Sulphur Springs home. I had not seen him for over a year, but he looked the same. Pale, dark hair, over six feet tall and lean to the point of emaciation, he peered down at me with milky brown eyes. I did not know his exact age, but a reasonable guess put him in his mid-forties.

"How's the job?" he asked, waving me toward an overstuffed leather couch.

"Same," I replied as I sat down, grateful for the coolness of the air conditioning. "No sleep, no cooperation, and no appreciation." Wade folded himself into his recliner, grabbed his remote off the nearby coffee table and muted the television. On his seventy inch screen, Jimmy Cagney continued to dance to the tune of Grand Old Flag in silence. Wade loved the classics.

"You're here about the disappearances...the three

David F. Gray

women," he said. I wasn't surprised. The case had made national headlines.

"All in their mid-thirties, all professional and all making good money. That's the only thing they have in common," I said. "The doctor is Hispanic, the hedge fund manager is Asian and the lawyer is Caucasian. They have no connections to each other. None of them have any family to speak of and there's no ransom demand."

"You've solved worse," Wade said pointedly.

"Given time, I can probably nail this one, especially with all the resources the Feds are pouring into the case."

"But you don't think there's time." I shook my head.

"I *know* there isn't. I think they might still be alive, but not for long." I looked him square in the eye. "Will you help?" Wade's nod was one part compassion and two parts resignation.

"Yeah," he said, holding out his right hand. "You know the drill." I took his hand and closed my eyes.

Once I had referred to Wade as a psychic. That had earned me a harsh glare and a stern warning not to call him that again...ever. I still don't understand what he does, but I know that it's real. Like I said, he's my edge.

He tried to explain it to me once. Somehow he can see the connections we make with other people, past, present or future. He could track my bloodline back to Adam, if he had a mind to, or track it through countless futures to the end of the world. Even the most ephemeral connection, living or dead, could be traced.

There was a good chance that, sometime in the future, I would come into contact with at least one of the three missing women, even if it meant finding their

Barriers

bodies lying in some back alley. If he could find that connection, then he could tag them and through them, their kidnappers. That might lead him to a location, and with a little luck we could change their fates.

I've used Wade on three other cases, and it was his lead that broke each case. He never accepts payment or credit. He only has two conditions. One, I only come to him when there are no other options and two, I never tell anyone else. He demands absolute secrecy. If I blab, our deal is off.

If he was poking around in my mind, I couldn't feel it. I gripped his hand for several minutes, kept my mouth shut and let him work. Two identical cases, one in Atlanta and one in Cincinnati, had ended with six dead, all women. I didn't know why the kidnapper had surfaced in Tampa, or even if it was the same person, but I had not been lying when I told Wade that time was running out. The last disappearance had occurred a week ago. In both the Atlanta and Cincinnati cases, all three women had been found dead ten days after the last one disappeared.

Time dragged on until at last Wade released my hand. When I opened my eyes and saw him staring back at me, I had to suppress a shudder. His emotions were running wild across his face, and the predominant emotion was terror. That scared me. In all the time I've known him, I've never seen Wade afraid.

"When this is over," he said in a low voice, "don't come looking for me. I won't be around."

"But…"

"I mean it, Eric. This is the last time I help you. I'm leaving town, probably tonight. Don't look for me. *Ever.* Understood?" I started to object, but that look in his eyes stopped me.

"All right," I said. Wade held my gaze for a moment, and then stood.

"We have to go now," he said, heading toward the front door. I didn't argue.

We got into my car and took off. Tampa isn't a small city and it's spread out over a fairly large area. There had not been any witnesses to the kidnappings, and all of the friends and co-workers were clean, so we had not been able to narrow our search to any particular area. Wade told me to head toward the dog track, about five miles from his house. He settled back into the seat and closed his eyes.

In the 1920s, Sulphur Springs had been an upper-class neighborhood, but time had taken its toll. The older houses were falling apart and the newer ones were small, barely adequate single family homes or cheaply made duplexes. Narrow streets, abandoned buildings, and roaming gangs made the area dangerous, especially at night.

It took less than five minutes to get to the dog track. The season had just ended and the hulking grandstand was dark and empty. I stopped when I got to the intersection of Waters and Kennedy, a four-lane street that ran past the track, and waited. I didn't have to wait long.

"Over there," said Wade, pointing. I followed his finger over to the old Sulphur Springs pool club.

"You sure?" He nodded. The pool club sat directly across from the dog track. In its heyday it had been a popular retreat, but it had been abandoned for decades. Local legend had it that the sulfur laden waters contained magical healing properties. A large two-story

Barriers

gazebo stood over the now capped spring. The upper floor had been host to numerous parties and other social functions. The lower level enclosed the spring.

Now the pool was filled with dark green rainwater, and the gazebo's white paint was faded and peeling. A sturdy chain link fence surrounded the pool, but the rest of the area lay open. A few scattered amber streetlights accented the glow of the full moon, providing adequate illumination. I eased my car onto Kennedy and turned towards the gazebo. Wade's hand shot out and grabbed me by the shoulder. "Stop here," he demanded.

"But…"

"I said *stop!*" I hit the brakes and pulled over to the curb. Wade was out of the car in an instant and I scrambled after him. His long stride forced me to jog to keep up. When we entered the empty parking lot that fronted the pool club, Wade pulled up. He stood there, staring at the gazebo. It shimmered softly with reflected moonlight, still a good fifty yards away. After a few moments, Wade pointed at the glowing structure.

"The girls are in there," he whispered, turning to face me. "Give me thirty seconds, no more. Then go in and *don't stop for anything.*" His hand shot out and gripped my shoulder with surprising strength. "They're still alive, but they're not alone. Do *not* hesitate. The men holding them have killed before and they'll kill again."

"I need to call for backup," I said, but Wade shook his head.

"No time. Now get ready. Do what you have to do, Eric." Licking my lips, I nodded. Wade released my arm and turned toward the gazebo.

"What are you going to…"

David F. Gray

"What I have to do, just like you," he replied, his voice shaking. "It doesn't concern you. Pray that it never does." And then he was gone. He angled off to the left, darting forward with nearly inhuman speed. Shoving my own fear into a small, dark corner of my mind, I started counting. When I reached thirty, I drew my Glock and started running.

It took another fifteen seconds to get across the parking lot. The bottom level of the gazebo was comprised of a series of columns and arches that held up the second floor. There were no doors, but the columns were at least five feet wide, blocking most of my view to the spring.

Halfway across the parking lot, I realized that there was a soft glow coming through the arches. *So much the better,* I thought as I reached the gazebo. The idea of going in blind did not sit well with me. I leaned against one of the columns, wasting a few precious seconds to catch my breath and wipe the sweat away from my forehead. Then, gripping my Glock with both hands, I stepped through the arch, and stopped dead in my tracks. I had steeled myself for just about anything...mutilated bodies, tortured, barely alive victims...anything. What I was not ready for was beauty... pure, absolute, perfect beauty.

In the center of the cement floor where the spring should have been, was a column of what could only be described as living light. Even now I cannot begin to describe it. I think it was maybe two feet wide, or maybe two miles, or two million miles. It penetrated the ceiling, the sky and for all I know the universe itself. I stared at the breathtaking sight before me, tears welling up in my eyes. I could sense that

Barriers

this...light...emanated from deep within the ground. It sparkled and danced within itself, glowing with every imaginable color along with an infinite number of unimaginable colors. Just to be near it made me feel whole and healed.

Fifteen years of police work had damaged me. I had seen more than one man should be allowed to see, but in just a few seconds I could feel the wounds from those years healing. I wanted to shout, to scream in ecstasy. To this day, I don't know exactly what I saw, but I know this. That indescribable column was alive, and it was aware. It sounds insane, but I felt as if I was staring at the very soul of the earth.

My hesitation nearly cost me my life.

ERIC!

Wade's shout tore through my mind, and *only* my mind, breaking the spell cast by the light. Stunned, I tore my eyes away. The expected obscenity presented itself.

The women were there, tied up and lying on the floor next to the light. Their clothes were ripped nearly to shreds, and in the glow I could easily see that they had been brutalized. They were bleeding from a dozen shallow cuts and their faces were bruised and swollen. They were tied together, arm to arm and ankle to ankle. It looked for all the world like some kind of pagan sacrifice.

Their tormenters were there as well. Both were male, Caucasian, middle aged, and dressed in black. By the time I spotted them, they had already seen me. The man closest to me, a hulking football lineman type well over six feet tall, had already drawn a long, serrated hunting knife and was coming straight at me. The other, small, thin and pale, remained where he was, hovering over his victims like some kind of deranged

Vulture. For just an instant, I saw tiny threads of light stretching out of the women and plunging into his chest. He in turn had threads reaching out of his forehead, stretching towards the light. But these threads were not made of light. They were dark. I looked at them and I saw corruption and death.

Wade had warned me not to hesitate, but if he had said nothing, I would still have fired. I think I would have fired even if that man had not drawn his knife. Something emanated from both of them that made me want to gag. It was a foul stench that was more spiritual than physical. I knew that, for the first time in my career, the first time in my *life*, I had come face to face with true evil.

My Glock bucked in my hand. I had a full clip and I divided eight slugs evenly between the two men; four shots each, straight to the chest. The noise reverberated through the gazebo. Both men went down without a sound. The threads joining the smaller man, the women and the light disappeared. I ejected the half empty clip and reloaded, just in case they had friends. I took a moment to make sure that both of them were dead. Then I checked the victims.

They were alive, and conscious. I used my pocketknife to cut their bounds and got them to their feet. They struggled to stand. All three were in deep shock. I was surprised that they made it to their feet, but looking back, I think that the light may have helped.

Ordinarily, I would have used my phone to call for an ambulance, but suddenly I knew that I had to get them away from the gazebo. Their kidnappers were dead, but there was something else close by. It was a presence, and like the light, it was aware. Unlike the light, it was *not* alive. I could feel it closing in, and if the darkness that had possessed the men had been bad, this was a thousand times worse.

I led the women through the nearest arch. Outside it was dead silent, but I could feel something closing in. I got the sense that there was a desperate battle being waged in and around the gazebo. It was like walking blindfolded through the middle of a battlefield.

Somehow I got the women back to my car, and it was only then that I felt safe enough to call for backup. Two of them seemed to be coming around, but the third had lapsed into unconsciousness.

I had three patrol units on scene in under two minutes, and a pair of ambulances there in ten. Fifteen minutes after that, my captain showed up with a forensics unit and a handful of F.B.I. agents in tow. The victims were taken away, and I spent the next few hours going over the night's events. I told the both the Feds and my captain that I had run down a dozen leads and one had finally panned out. I kept Wade out of it. I felt guilty, taking credit that belonged to him, but a promise is a promise.

I wasn't surprised to find that the marvelous column of light was gone when I got back to the gazebo. The bodies were still there, of course. They were never identified, and because of that, the case is still open.

There was just a hint of light in the eastern sky when we wrapped things up. I would be going on administrative leave because of the shootings, but I wasn't worried. In every conceivable way they were justified. The last patrol unit pulled away and I got into my own car. I still had at least an hour of paperwork waiting for me at the station. I wanted to get it done and go home, hug my wife and kids and sleep for a month. Just as I started the car, the passenger door opened, and Wade slid in. I looked at him, my face asking a hundred questions. He shook his head adamantly.

"Believe me Eric," he said, "the less you know, the better." I took a closer look at him. His face was drawn and haggard, as if he had aged ten years in a matter of hours. He held his right arm with his left, wincing in pain.

"Wade…"

"You got them out," he said. "That's the important thing. The rest…" His voice trailed off.

"That light," I whispered, and he smiled sadly at me.

"There are beautiful things in this world, Eric; powerful, pure, beautiful things. And there are forces that want nothing more than to destroy them." He licked his lips. "You've come close to something tonight, and you don't want to come any closer." His eyes bored into mine. "Because if you do," he said, and now his voice was made of steel, "it will cost you everything...your family, your career...*everything*." He looked back at the gazebo. "Walk away, Eric. Please, walk away." And with that, he got out of the car.

That was over three years ago. Since then, Sulphur Springs has experienced a bit of a renaissance. The pool has been renovated and the gazebo has been remodeled and painted. I stop by every now and then and watch the locals have a blast in the water. But I don't go near the gazebo.

True to his word, Wade disappeared. The women recovered, physically at least. They'll be dealing with

Barriers

the mental and emotional scars for the rest of their lives, but they *are* alive. That has to count for something. The Feds took over the case, and last I heard they haven't made any headway. I got a commendation and a promotion, and I've been very careful to heed Wade's advice. I walked away from a mystery that night, and I continue to walk away. I have a good life and I intend to keep it.

Sometimes, late at night when my family is asleep, I step outside. Every so often, I fancy that I can see dark shapes hiding in the shadows, or a faint glow of perfect light hovering at the edge of my vision. I tell myself that it is a trick of the moonlight. Most of the time, I believe it. The other times…

I can't get that light out of my head. I can see it in my dreams. I can feel it in my heart. It's out there, somewhere, everywhere. Its beauty and strength constantly tug at me. I'm terrified that someday I'll answer its call walk away from my life. I'll begin a quest that will take me out of sight and possibly even out of memory. Perhaps I'll find that light again, but maybe I'll stumble across the creatures that only live to corrupt it. If that happens…

No. I'm going to keep my life. I'm going to hang on to it with every fiber of my being. I don't know what kind of battle Wade fought that night, but it's not my fight. My battle is on the streets of Tampa, going after ordinary thieves, murderers and drug dealers.

It's not my fight.

Dear God, don't let it ever be my fight.

David F. Gray

Mamaw's Beast

I stood in front of the old Independence house, trying to layer the memories of a long dead childhood over the reality of the present. There had been changes, of course. I knew that there would be, after nearly fifty years.

In my memory I saw a large, two-story wood-frame house with white walls, bright green shutters and a wide front porch. The house I was looking at was much smaller. Time does that, I guess. The walls were still white, although the paint was blistered and faded, and most of the shutters were missing. The gravel driveway had been paved with cement, and the huge oak tree that had once shaded the wide front yard was long gone.

The Beast was still there.

Five decades ago, it had risen out of the cellar, although that was never its true home. It was my grandmother who recognized it for what it was. It had stolen something precious from her, but she was a tough old bird. She knew things...secret things...and she was not without power. For almost two years, they fought. She had managed to hurt it, but in the end it killed her. After that, we moved out.

I stared at the old house, letting my memories flow. The Independence of 1964 had been a typical small country town. About twenty miles south of Cincinnati, it sat in the Kentucky high country, surrounded by tree covered rolling hills. There had been a drug store, complete with a marble soda fountain, a barber shop, a hardware store and two small grocery stores.

A Walgreens had replaced old man Henderson's

Barriers

drug store. The barber shop was closed and boarded over, and the hardware store had been put out of business by the Home Depot franchise that occupied several acres on the other side of town. Still, the old town had the same sleepy quality I remembered as a child.

The earthy aromas of the country washed over me as I stood next to my BMW. It was late in May and the honeysuckles were in full bloom. Their sweet scent complimented the smell of manure from the cow pasture a quarter mile away. I jammed my hands into my pockets and walked past the house into the back yard. Like the house, it was smaller than I remembered, but essentially the same, although the garden that once supplied my family with fresh corn, tomatoes, string beans, carrots and potatoes was now an empty, weed infested plot of land next to the free-standing garage. Visions of countless birthday parties, potluck picnics and winter sleigh rides piled into my mind.

The memories grew so thick that I felt as if I was smothering under their weight. I returned to the front yard and stepped up onto the porch. The wood creaked under my weight. As promised, the key was hanging on a nail next to the front door. *Country folk,* I thought, shaking my head. Even in this day and age, it seemed that the citizens of Independence left their doors and windows unlocked. With a last glance over my shoulder, I opened the door and went inside. My vision blurred. I staggered, as if the floor suddenly buckled. The last thing I remember was falling.

* * *

David F. Gray

When I came to, I was lying on the hard wooden floor, staring up at the plaster ceiling. I had fallen hard, banging the back of my head. I groaned and gingerly prodded the large lump that had formed there. Wincing at the pain, I sat up and tried to make sense of the world. *Why did I come here? Why?* The question rattled around in my mind, but I knew the answer. I had been *compelled* to come here, just as I had been compelled to buy the vacant house. Behind me, the door was still open. It had been mid-afternoon when I had arrived, but now it was dusk outside. The small living room was shrouded in shadows. I squinted at my watch and saw that over three hours had passed.

I desperately *needed* to leave. Scrambling to my feet, I stumbled outside and stood on the porch. The crickets were in the middle of their nightly serenade, and it seemed as if a million fireflies were hovering over the front yard, flashing on and off like twitchy Christmas lights. I stared at them for a long time, willing myself to get into the car. I don't know how long I stood there...certainly long enough for the evening light to fade completely... but eventually I went back inside.

There was no power, but there was ample moonlight streaming through the wide living and dining room windows. The floor creaked under my feet as I went into the kitchen. It was pretty much as I remembered it. I turned around, and in a single heartbeat, forty years rewound and a memory, long repressed, lit up inside of my mind.

I see myself sitting on the kitchen floor, playing with my wooden blocks. Dad was at work, and Mom and Mamaw were down in the cellar, canning vegetables.

Barriers

Mom calls for me to bring her a glass of water and a clean towel. I grab both and start down the stairs. The next thing I remember is Mamaw carrying me back into the kitchen. I was screaming, my face bright red with the effort. Mom is right behind, yelling at Mamaw to put me down. Mamaw sits me on one of the kitchen chairs and kneels in front of me. Her blue eyes are twin pinpoints of fire. Looking into them, I feel as if I am burning.

I snapped back into the present, shaken by the vivid memory. That was the moment, I knew. That was when Mamaw became aware of the Beast.

Now, the door to the cellar was shut and latched. Just to the right of it was the staircase that led up to three bedrooms and a single bathroom. I stared at the door, unwilling to move. I was sure that the Beast would hear me. It was down there. After all this time, it was still there, waiting.

It took a long time. Finally, keeping my eyes off the door, I eased across the kitchen and went upstairs. At the top, I took a quick look around and then went into my old bedroom. Everything was the same, and yet it was all different. The small closet, the big windows, the high ceiling; it took several seconds, but I finally managed to pull the pieces together and remember the place I had spent a large portion of my childhood. I opened the windows and let in the night air.

Downstairs, the cellar door rattled. I froze, knowing that I was trapped. There were only two ways out of the house, and they both ran straight past that door. It rattled again and then opened with a long, high-pitched squeak. I stumbled over to the far corner of the room and slid to the floor, wrapping my arms around my knees. The Beast was coming for me.

The stairs began to creak, as if bearing a heavy weight. Then the noise stopped abruptly at what I thought might have been halfway up to where I crouched. A moment later, three rapid squeaks sounded out. The Beast retreated. I heard it moving about in the kitchen until, after an eternity, the cellar door opened and closed.

I stayed in my room the rest of the night. All was quiet, but I fancied that I could hear the beast moving about the cellar. Again, I tried to force myself out of the house. I desperately wanted to go back to New York and reclaim my old life, but the insidious power that had compelled me to leave my adopted city and return to the place of my birth now compelled me to remain in that house. I cowered in the corner, and sometime around four in the morning fatigue won out over terror and I dozed off.

The movers arrived the next day. For a while, I was able to forget about the previous night as I arranged my furniture. The power company called to let me know that there had been a mix up and that they would not be out for another two days. I blew up over this. The girl, Charlene was her name, tried to stay calm, but I'm good with words, especially when I'm mad. I had her in tears by the time I was through. I ended the call and threw my cell phone across the room. Then I stormed out the front door. I decided that I would find a motel near I-75 and spend the night. In the morning, I would leave Independence forever.

I stepped off the porch and gasped. My eyes blurred and I could not breathe. My heart thudded against my chest and, for a moment, I was sure that I was having a

Barriers

heart attack. I groped my way back into the house and slumped down onto the living room floor. The Beast had made it clear. I was not going anywhere.

That night I lay in my bed, waiting. Around three, I heard the cellar door shake. Then the latch fell away and it creaked open. Footsteps sounded through the kitchen and into the living room. For over an hour the Beast wandered through the first floor, knowing full well that it was tormenting me. Finally, it started upstairs. I counted the squeaks, and when it had almost reached the top, it stopped. It waited there for a long time. Then, as if deciding to prolong my agony, it returned to the cellar.

I got up at daybreak and for some insane reason, opened the cellar door. I peered into the darkness, wondering just what I was doing. The damp, cold, stale air made me shiver. I must have blacked out for a second. I blinked, and found myself halfway down the stairs. With a whimper, I scrambled back into the light. The rest of the day I spent moving about the house. I could not remain in any single place, and I could not leave. The Beast's hold on me was now so strong that I could not even step out onto the porch.

The third night came and I went to my bed. The hours dragged on and eventually I fell into a fitful sleep. Suddenly a loud thud rattled the house. I jerked awake, heart pounding. The stairs creaked and groaned, and I realized that the thud had been the cellar door slamming open. The gloves were off. The Beast had finished teasing me. It was coming.

I counted the squeaks, and at twelve I knew that the Beast had reached the top. Harsh gray moonlight was coming through the windows, bathing everything in a surreal glow. A shadow fell across my bedroom door. I stared at it, unable to scream. The shadow moved. It entered the bedroom and glided over to where I lay. Then it sat down on the bed. I felt the mattress move and heard the bed frame creak. I stared at the apparition, if apparition it was. Its hair was pulled back into a tight bun, and its skin was wrinkled with the weight of years. Its face turned toward me, and even in the darkness I recognized its features.

"Mamaw," I whispered. The apparition nodded. I think she smiled. "Mamaw, is it you?" My grandmother nodded again. Then she reached out and touched my arm. Her skin was warm and dry, and the touch comforted rather than frightened me.

My fear vanished. The Beast was gone! Somehow, my Mamaw's spirit had exorcised it from the house. I was free! I reached out for her, but she stood and walked over to the door, beckoning for me to follow her. There was no way that I could refuse her. I was on my feet in an instant, following her dark form downstairs.

The cellar door was still open and she went through it. I hesitated, but her call was too strong. Groping in the darkness, I felt my way down the stairs. There was just a hint of light coming from the window wells over the stationary tubs. It was a small space, only about fifteen feet long and twenty feet wide. The handmade wooden shelves that had once held dozens of mason jars filled with preserved fruits and vegetables were in front of me. Behind me were the stationary tubs where Mom and Mamaw had done the laundry. The sup pump stood alone to my right, silent in the dry season, and the furnace squatted in the opposite corner. I was barefoot

Barriers

and shirtless, wearing only sweatpants. The dirt floor was cold and rough against my bare feet.

Another memory tickled the back of my thoughts. It felt important, and I tried to draw it out, but it flittered away. I could now sense a great barrier deep in my mind, blocking something that I desperately needed. I tried to breech it again, but it held firm.

Mamaw stood in front of me. She took my hand and led me behind the shelves. Understand, there *was* no 'behind'. The shelves were flush against the cellar wall, but when she drew me over, I saw a narrow crawlspace, barely a foot wide. It was both real and not real, and the effect was quite disorienting. At her silent command, I got down on all fours and began to crawl. The grainy dirt bit into my hands and feet.

I squeezed into the narrow there/not there space. A few feet in, I discovered a tunnel. The opening was small, perhaps only a yard or so square...just big enough for me to crawl into. The tunnel burrowed into the back wall, disappearing into the darkness. Again, memory tugged at me, but I ignored it. I hunkered down and went in.

I don't know how long I crawled. The tunnel twisted and turned so many times that I was soon confused beyond hope. The darkness was complete; a palpable, irresistible weight pressing down on me, threatening to crush me out of existence. I kept going deeper and deeper into the earth, heedless of whether or not I would be able to get back to the cellar. Part of me knew that this tunnel could not exist, just as a part of me knew that it did. As I continued forward, I was assailed by one undeniable fact. *I had come this way before.*

I could feel the memories now, dammed up behind

the barrier in my mind. Soon, I knew that barrier would shatter and I would remember. Until then, all I could do was keep crawling.

I came upon the end of the tunnel unexpectedly. I felt, rather than saw, the sides fall away. I reached above me and felt nothing but cool air. Cautiously I stood and found that I was in a dry open space. There was a rustle behind me, and I knew that Mamaw had arrived. I could not picture her crawling through the tunnel, but it did not matter. I felt safe with her there. After all, she had vanquished the Beast.

Light blazed up, blinding me. I cried out, covering my eyes. There was no sound, but the light seemed to come at me from all directions. It ripped at me, its very essence assaulting me from every side. It *hurt*. I tried to squint through my fingers. My eyes adjusted a little, and I could see that I was in some kind of dome or rotunda, about fifty feet in diameter and maybe twenty feet high. The walls were red stone, rough hewn and covered with symbols that I almost recognized.

"Mamaw," I cried out again, desperately trying to find her in the blazing light. Suddenly my skin began to smolder, and I screamed from the pain.

"Now, demon, you will pay." Her voice was harsh and inhuman. It reverberated off the walls of the rotunda and I screamed again. I whirled around, uncovering my eyes, and found the source of light. Mamaw stood behind me, blazing with a power that I could not bear to look at...*and a power that I recognized*. Her eyes were aflame with fire. Her mouth opened impossibly wide, and her voice blasted at me from every direction. The smell of my burning flesh rose to choke me.

Barriers

"Mamaw!"

"Silence demon," she shouted, and I felt my tongue cleave to the roof of my mouth. "You will not call me that. You will not dare defile that name." Invisible hands grabbed me and I was flung against the far wall of the rotunda. The stone itself burned me. I tried to scream again, but my mouth would not open. Mamaw glided forward.

"Now, at last," she said in that awful booming voice, "I have you. By the power of your enemy and my ally, I bind you forever." Invisible fetters clamped themselves on my arms and legs, pinning me to the wall. Unbreakable yet invisible chains wrapped themselves around my torso, squeezing me so hard that I was sure that I was going to be cut in half.

"Mamaw! *Please.*"

"I said be silent! There is the only one who had the right to call me by that name. You took him. He was the most precious thing in my life, and you *devoured* him." The barrier in my mind cracked and splintered. In an instant, memories long repressed returned. I remembered who I was. I remembered *what* I was.

I was immortal. I was forever.

I was the Beast.

I was from beyond...beyond the world, beyond the universe, beyond reality itself. I was as far above the pathetic creatures that roamed this ball of mud as they were above the worms that crawled within it. I was nearly all powerful, but...

The last piece of my memory snapped into place. I had a great enemy. We had fought beyond time and space. I was defeated. I was chased across creation itself until I was caught. I was crushed, *compacted*, and imprisoned in this very rotunda. My nearly infinite power was stripped away.

I remembered millennia of scraping and scratching at my prison walls, seeking a way out. My enemy had beaten me, but had been weakened by our fight. My prison was not perfect. Finally, I found a crack, the tiniest of flaws. Through it, I found a small town, a small house, and a small boy. I called to him, led him to this prison, and then slowly consumed his soul. I used his body to escape my bonds.

But something went wrong. The boy's memories, his thoughts, his *heart*, were strong. The longer I lived in his body, the more I became him. My...*his*... parents never suspected, but Mamaw knew. She bided her time until, just after my twelfth birthday, she made her move. She almost succeeded, but I remembered just enough of my true self to destroy her. Even so, her final blow had been her most devastating. In a single deft move, she had managed to block my true memories behind the barrier I had only just now sensed. For all intents and purposes, I had become the boy.

Mamaw never gave up, not even in death. Her spirit hovered in the Independence house for decades, patiently waiting, growing stronger with each passing year. She kept the house from being destroyed just as she kept anyone from living in it. Finally, she drew me back. Now, she had me.

I strained against my bonds. Mamaw stared at me, and the power within her seared me. I recognized it for what it was. Somehow she had forged an alliance with my enemy. I cried out, begging her for mercy.

"Did you have mercy on my baby?" Her voice cut and flayed me. "No, you will never take another soul,

Barriers

demon. If there truly is a final judgment, and if there is any justice, it will be my hand that delivers you into oblivion. Until then, may you rot in this prison."

I screamed again. My body burst into flame, and I felt my human shell disintegrate. I was my true self once more. A look of utter satisfaction crossed the old woman's face, and I saw peace replace her pain. Then she was gone. Darkness filled my prison. I was alone.

And here I have stayed. Hatred and rage consume me. I strain at my bonds, but they do not give. I am trapped, just as I had been trapped for so many thousands of years. For a long time, I struggle. Then I settle down. I have escaped before. I will escape again.

I begin to chip at my fetters. Sooner or later, they will weaken and break. I will find another soul to take, and once again I will walk the earth. I have time. I have all the time in the world.

David F. Gray

The Vampires Are Always Guilty

The call came through at precisely 10:14 p.m. A sixty-year-old male was unconscious and lying face down in the street. He was alive, at least he was when the frantic passerby phoned it in, but he was bleeding from the neck. An ambulance was on its way and my partner and I were the lucky ones to get the call. I read the address off the small screen in our unmarked car and groaned. My new partner, Randall Pink, raised his eyebrows in the obvious question.

"Benny and Larry," I said, closing my eyes. "God, sometimes you can just feel a crappy shift coming."

"Regulars?" I could hear the tension in his voice. Randall had been promoted to detective six months ago and had way too much to learn. It was my unhappy job to train him.

"Oh yeah," I said. I opened the glove compartment, grabbed a spare clip that I kept for special occasions such as this, and loaded it into my .45. "Let's roll."

Benny's small single-story house was just two streets over. By the time we got there, the ambulance was already on the scene. I checked in with the paramedics, just in case the poor guy was conscious. One of them recognized me.

"Detective Stabler," she said, nodding.

"June," I replied. "How is he?"

"Unconscious but stable," said June. "He's lost a lot of blood." I glanced over at Benny's house. Sure enough, I could see him peeking out from behind the curtain.

"I need to take a look," I muttered. June made an

Barriers

'after you' gesture and we climbed into the ambulance. The old man was lying on a stretcher. Another medic was tending to him, but he moved aside and let me examine the twin puncture marks on his neck.

"Was he turned?" I asked. June shook her head.

"He was fed on, but he didn't feed."

"Then he'll live?"

"Most likely. They'll keep him in intensive care for a few days, but he should pull through." She glanced at Benny's house. "You gonna talk to them?"

"What do you think? Of course I'm going to talk to them." June shifted her eyes to Randall.

"Does he know?"

"Know what?" This was from Randall.

"Not yet," I said, ignoring the rookie. June grinned.

"Wish I could watch." She waved at the victim. "If you've seen enough, we need to transport him."

"Go ahead," I said. "I'll get his statement when he wakes up, not that it will do much good." June got the old man secured in the back of the ambulance while Randall and I headed toward Benny's house.

"What was that all about?" asked Randall.

"You'll see," I answered.

"But…"

"I said you'll see," I snapped. "There's a reason why I was picked to train you. There's stuff they don't teach you at the academy or as a beat cop. It's stuff that even old farts like me don't like to talk about. This is some of that stuff. Now keep your mouth shut and your eyes open."

We stepped up to Benny's front door and I rang the bell. After a moment, the door slowly opened with a loud creak. Beyond it was only darkness.

"Who dares disturb my slumber?" The voice was cold and dead.

"Knock it off, Benny," I snapped. "I've got an impossible caseload, my shift just started and already you're giving me a headache." A light snapped on and Benny stepped into view. Randall let out a yelp and stumbled backward. Benny eyed him with a mixture of humor and disdain.

"Who's the kid?" he asked.

"My new partner," I answered.

"I'm sorry," replied Benny. I really think he meant it. I glanced over my shoulder at Randall, who had drawn his Glock and was pointing it straight at Benny's heart.

"Stop that," I said, exasperated. "We don't shoot suspects. Besides, that toy won't do you any good. You'll just piss him off." Randall stared at our prime suspect, his eyes wide with both terror and loathing. I understood, of course. Benny was tall, well over six feet, and bald as a cantaloupe. His wrinkled skin was gray. I don't mean that it had a gray tint to it. It was gray; battleship gray to be precise. His eyes were jet black with no trace of white. His red lips were thin and pressed together. He looked like a frail old man well into his nineties, but I knew for a fact that he was a lot older and not so frail.

I had known Benny since my first month as a detective and even now I found him more than a little terrifying, although the tattered baby blue robe he was wearing offset his sinister appearance. The fact that it was embroidered with tiny yellow ducks helped.

"Uh...uh...Dan?"

"Yes, Randall," I said in a low tone reserved for

Barriers

slow elementary school students. "Benny is a vampire. He drinks the blood of his victims and he can change into a bat, a wolf or sometimes when the mood hits him, a glowing mist." I thought Randall's eyes were going to bulge out of his head and wondered briefly if that was the way I looked when my old partner introduced me to our local undead citizens all those years ago.

"You're here about the old man," said Benny. I could hear the resignation in his voice.

"Yep," I said. "You know the drill. I've got to talk to Larry as well."

"Come on in then," sighed Benny. He moved aside and I stepped through the door. A second later, I realized that I was alone and turned to face Randall.

"Well?" Randall's face went through an amazing array of expressions. Then he surprised me by holstering his weapon and following me inside.

Benny's home was eerily ordinary. A red, overstuffed couch covered by a hand knit blue afghan dominated the small living room, while battered wooden furniture accented the faded yellow wallpaper. Two cast iron lamps with dusty lampshades provided the light. The only thing that did not seem old was the newspaper lying half open on the couch. Randall surveyed the room with obvious surprise. Benny noticed, of course.

"What did you expect?" he demanded. "Piles of bones? Blood drenched coffins?"

"Relax kid," I said. "He keeps all that stuff downstairs."

"Oh…good." Randall was barely holding it together.

"I'm joking, kid," I said. I asked Benny, "Where's

Larry?"

"Here." The voice came from the couch. Now it was my turn to jump. The couch was empty.

"Larry?"

"What?"

"What the heck are you playing at?" There was a shimmer in the air, and Larry appeared. At least, he sort of appeared. I could see right through him. Behind me, Randall made a gagging sound.

"Good God, man. What happened?"

"I'll tell you what happened," snapped Benny. "Some punk kid got lucky. Staked my poor Larry while he was out a few nights ago." The newspaper rustled as Larry got up and floated over to where Benny stood. Benny tried to put his arm around him, but his hand passed right through his shoulders.

"It's not so bad," said Larry in a hollow voice. "We've dealt with worse. We can deal with this." Benny smiled gently.

"I still love you. It doesn't matter to me what form you take." Randall hiccupped. I glanced at him and shrugged.

"They're lovers," I said casually. "Have been ever since I've known them."

"Gay...vampires," whispered Randall. He was struggling, but he was still conscious. That put him two steps ahead of the last partner I trained.

"All vampires are gay, or rather, bi-sexual," I said. "They feed off both men and women and derive sexual pleasure from both." I turned my attention back to Benny. "I thought you were on the wagon," I said.

"Yep," said Benny. "I have been for decades. No human blood for me; only cows and an occasional dog

Barriers

or cat." Randall gagged some more.

"The victim was bitten by a vampire," I said. "That means you, Benny. Only you, since Larry bit the big one." I winced at my own poor taste. "Sorry. That was uncalled for."

"I should hope so," said Benny. "And we're not the only undead in the city."

"But you are the only undead in this precinct," I said. "I seriously doubt if anyone in the Martinus clan is going to come this far to feed. You're going to have to do better than that."

"I can," said Benny. He opened his mouth wide, impossibly wide for a human. His exposed teeth gleamed in the dim light. "Ake a ook."

"Excuse me?"

"I aid, ake a ook." I got it.

I didn't want to. Vampires smell of rotting things. Still, I did as Benny asked. I leaned forward and immediately saw what he wanted me to see. His fangs, along with most of his teeth, were gone. Only gaping, empty sockets remained.

"What the hell?"

"Oooth eecay."

"What?" Benny closed his mouth again.

"Tooth decay," he said.

"Ridiculous. Vampires don't get tooth decay," I said.

"Of course we do," said Benny. "People think we're immortal, but even for us time eventually takes its toll. I'm very old, Detective. Now, I eat the old-fashioned way, through a straw."

"And I don't have a physical body anymore," said Larry. "I suck lifeforce."

"Excuse me?"

"I live off the energy of other living things. And don't give me that look, Detective. I haven't sucked a human since I got staked. Usually it's dogs, although yesterday I sucked a cat." I stifled a groan, knowing that that mental image would be rattling around inside my head for a long time.

"So you see, Detective," said Benny, "we are innocent." He smiled his dead smile. "Maybe it was a werewolf."

"A werewolf?" Randall's voice was about an octave above its normal range.

"Relax kid," said Larry. "Benny's just yanking your chain. Werewolves are a myth."

"Huh?"

"A myth. They don't exist."

"You're a ghost," said Randall. Larry shrugged.

"So?"

"And you're a vampire." This was to Benny.

"What's your point?" said Benny. I could see that he was losing patience.

"You said that werewolves are a myth."

"Yeah?"

"But you're a vampire."

"What are you implying?"

"You're a vampire." Benny shook his head.

"You've really got that Abbot and Costello thing going, Detective," he said.

"Come on partner," I said, steering Randall toward the door. "We got what we need."

"But…but…but…"

"I know," I said sympathetically. "Don't worry. If it makes you feel any better, this is the hard part." I

Barriers

steered Randall out of the house. Benny shut the door behind us and we made our way back to our squad car. I opened the door for Randall and then gave Benny's house one last glance. Something was bothering me, but I could not put my finger on it. There was Benny peeking out of one window and Larry peeking out of the other. I waved at them and they disappeared.

"The vampires are always guilty," I muttered.

"Huh?" Randall was still dazed, but he was coming around.

"Something my old partner once told me. If there are bite marks on the victims, then the vampires are always guilty."

"Oh. Of course. Bite marks always mean vampires. That makes perfect sense." I gave Randall an encouraging nod.

"Keep at it, kid," I said. "You'll get there." I shut his door and walked around to the driver's side. I started to get in, but froze. My mind revved into high gear and played back our entire visit in a few seconds. I remembered how Larry had materialized out of thin air. He had floated over to Benny, *and the newspaper had rustled as he left the couch.*

"Come on, kid," I said. I ran back toward Benny's house. Randall got out of the car and hurried after me.

"What?" he panted as he caught up.

"We got played," I said. "Stay close. This might get ugly." We reached the door and I drew my .45. Then I lunged against the door. It flew open and there, in the living room, were my two favorite vampires. Larry, as solid as they come, was holding Benny to his bare chest. Benny's mouth was latched on to Larry's right nipple. Bright red blood was seeping out from his lips. I had caught them red handed. They flew apart. Larry fell back onto the couch while poor Benny landed on the floor. Benny's robe flapped open, burning yet another unspeakable image into my brain. Both vampires tried to look indignant, but I had them and they knew it.

"I gotta hand it to you, Larry," I said. "That's an amazing amount of control you have over your mist form. You really had me believing that you were a ghost. It must have taken you years to perfect the technique."

"Centuries," growled Larry. "What tipped you off?"

"When you floated over to Benny the newspaper moved. The last I heard, a ghost can't affect the physical world, at least not without a great deal of effort."

"You mean that he's not a ghost?" squeaked Randall. I shook my head.

"Nope. Just a plain old everyday vampire, and the vampires are always guilty."

"Hey," exclaimed Benny. "I don't appreciate being profiled."

"File a complaint," I retorted.

"You know that I'll have to kill you now," said Benny, getting to his feet. "But I think I'll turn your partner."

"Uh uh," I said, cocking my .45. "Stay there, Benny." Despite our long history, I had never pointed my gun at him before. Being what he was, it didn't bother him at all.

"Sorry Detective," said Benny. "I like you. You've always given us a fair shake, but I can't have it known that we're feeding on human blood again." He glided toward me. I aimed, fired, and hit him right in the heart.

Barriers

Benny smiled.

"After all these years, you really should know better," he said. I nodded.

"Actually, I do." I wiggled my gun. "Special bullets, made from petrified wood and blessed by a local priest. It's something we just started experimenting with at the precinct. Theoretically, they should be a lot more effective than an old-fashioned stake." Benny took another step toward me, but suddenly his feet began to dissolve into dust. He looked down with a mixture of horror and amazement as his body disintegrated. "Looks like theory just became fact," I said.

"Benny?" Larry rushed to him. I took advantage of the distraction and pumped two shots into him. Within seconds, both vampires were nothing more than piles of dust on the floor.

"Sorry guys," I said. "But you know the rules." I turned and walked out of the house. Randall followed, breathing hard.

"Larry wasn't a ghost," he panted as we headed toward the car.

"Good, kid," I muttered.

"Then how…"

"Benny wasn't kidding about his fangs," I said. "They were gone. The only way he could eat was to have Larry feed him."

"So…"

"So Larry would feed off a normal human, store the blood in his own body, and then feed Benny. Hmmm. I wonder how he managed to hold on to it while he was in mist form? That must have taken some serious practice."

"Oh."

"You all right, kid?" There was no answer. I turned just in time to see Randall heave his last meal across the sidewalk. I gave him time to get himself back together. Then I got him back into the car and we headed downtown. I had a very unofficial report to file with my captain. On the upside, the new bullets worked just fine. They would certainly be needed. There were rumors that some of the other clans in the city were growing restless.

"So that's it?" asked Randall. "They're gone?" I shook my head.

"Nah. They'll be back. Vampires always come back. I think it's a rule or something. Some idiot with a spell book will probably conjure them into this world again. I give it about a year before they're back in the neighborhood."

"And we'll have to do this all over again?"

"Well, they might behave. You never know. At any rate, no, *we* won't be doing this again. *You* will. I'm retiring as soon as you're up to speed." I glanced over at him. "So what have we learned tonight?" I asked. He thought about it for long seconds.

"The vampires are always guilty," he said finally. I nodded, satisfied.

"Yep."

One Perfect Moment

The mobile on my nightstand trilled at just past one in the morning, dragging me out of a fitful sleep. I grabbed it, noted the caller ID, and thumbed the 'receive' button.

"What?" I mumbled, trying to sound annoyed.

"Kurt? Sorry to wake you."

"S'alright," I yawned. "I had to answer the phone anyway."

"Funny. Look, you alone?" He knew the answer, of course. The entire news staff at WFAC had watched sympathetically as my marriage of eleven years had tanked. Karen had taken the kids and the house. I got a beat-up Mustang and a one-bedroom apartment in one of Tampa's less desirable neighborhoods. John Roland was the news director... my boss and my friend...and he also knew that even though Karen and I had been divorced for over six months, I still could not bring myself to sleep with another woman.

"Yeah. What's up?"

"Plenty. Terrell's sick, and Jack is in Miami on assignment. I know you put in a long weekend, but things are happening fast and I need my top videographer."

"Flatterer," I said, coming fully awake. "Give me fifteen minutes."

"Make it ten," he answered, and hung up. My apartment was just two blocks away from the station. I threw on some semi-clean clothes, brushed my teeth, splashed some water in my face and made it in eight minutes flat.

David F. Gray

I walked into a newsroom alive with activity. Three major stories had broken in the past thirty minutes, and most of the news staff had been called in to augment the night crew. I tried to look grumpy but failed. I get double time for extra work, and triple if I have to go in harm's way. Child support adds up, and besides, I hate sleeping alone.

A coast guard helicopter had crashed into Tampa Bay during a rescue mission. To the north, a tractor-trailer had overturned on the I-4 interchange, demolishing an overpass. Finally, there had been a fatal stabbing at a local church. Three men were down, including the resident priest. Two were confirmed dead while the priest was barely hanging on. Being the senior videographer, the choice was mine and I picked the church. Shooting on the water is a pain, and the truck crash, while no doubt spectacular, was hardly national news. I wasn't pursuing a network job but it never hurts to get a little national exposure. A murder in a church had a good chance to make it to a CNN or at least MSNBC. Not only that, but the tip had come from one of our many sources, not through official channels. We had a shot of beating the other stations to the scene.

Kelly Preston was assigned as reporter. African American, pretty, and a bundle of energy, she was fresh out of her college internship and determined to make a name for herself. WFAC was her first job in the industry. We signed out a van and headed for Saint Francis, a Catholic church about ten minutes away. By the time we got there, the bright yellow 'police line-do not cross' tapes were already in place, but no other news vehicles were in sight. I parked across the street

Barriers

and we got to work.

Saint Francis is a petite but elegant church, a fifty-year-old single-story structure constructed with large gray granite blocks that looked sturdy enough to withstand a Category Four hurricane. From what we could gather over the police band, a suspect was already in custody. The priest had been airlifted to Tampa General.

The coroner's van was parked in front of the church, which meant that the bodies were still inside. Forensics would be busy collecting evidence. We would not be allowed access to the crime scene until both victims were removed.

There were two uniformed officers standing outside the church and I knew them both by sight. Over the years, I've managed to develop a fairly decent working relationship with the Tampa PD. While Kelly was getting herself together, I grabbed my camera and walked over to the officers, grabbing some exterior shots of the church on the way. One of them, a rookie whose name I could not remember, nodded at me. The other, a ten-year veteran named Jim Mallory, waved me over.

"So, they dragged you out of bed," he said.

"Yeah," I answered. "It's amazing what I'll do for a little overtime."

"You'll earn it tonight," said Jim, nodding toward the church entrance. "It's ugly in there." I had a short window of opportunity. Other news crews would be arriving within minutes.

"How ugly?"

"Very," said Jim. "A man and woman, multiple stab wounds and gutted from throat to crotch. It's as bad as

I've ever seen."

"We heard you had a perp."

"Just left," Jim replied. "He should be processed in a couple of hours. They'll walk him then." That meant that we would shoot him walking. It was going to be a long night and a tight deadline. I glanced over at the rookie and saw that he was staring across the street. Turning, I saw Kelly coming toward us. She looked a little miffed, probably because she thought I was doing her job. I was, but she knew better than to make a scene in the field.

"Hi," she said to Jim as she approached. "Kelly Preston, WFAC news." Her delivery was friendly, professional and just a little funny. I glanced over at Jim and saw him hiding a smile. He recognized a newbie when he saw one.

At that instant, the front doors of the church banged open and the first of two stretchers rolled out. I left Kelly with Jim and the rookie, shouldered my camera and started shooting. The bodies were completely covered, but the black body bags made for some fairly dramatic video.

By the time they had been loaded into the coroner's van, teams from some of the other local stations were on the scene. Reporters were busy asking questions and my own counterparts were shooting anything and everything in sight. An hour after we arrived, the detective in charge came out and gave a statement, informing us of what we already knew. This was indeed a triple homicide. Two of the victims had been pronounced dead on site, and the third, the priest, had passed away thirty minutes ago. A suspect was in custody and we could all get a look at him in about an

Barriers

hour. Then, under close supervision, he allowed us access to the crime scene.

It *was* ugly. The stabbings had taken place in the front of the church, just below the altar. Three large pools of blood had formed on the floor, soaking into the thick blue carpet. Two short phrases had been scrawled onto the altar itself, using that same blood. *The damned are here,* said one. *We are patient,* said the other. The second phrase sent a chill up my spine. *We*. It was a distinct possibility that this murderer had one or more accomplices.

I got my shots of the altar and then concentrated on the rest of the sanctuary. Despite its impressive exterior, the inside of Saint Francis was fairly bland. Big enough to seat maybe a hundred people, it had a low, vaulted ceiling, cheap looking chandeliers, two rows of sturdy wooden pews and nondescript white walls. There wasn't even any stained glass. The only real decoration was a six-by-four-foot reprint hanging on one wall to the right of the altar. I didn't know the artist, but I recognized the work. It depicted Adam and Eve being driven out of Eden by an angel wielding a flaming sword. I shot it and headed back outside to where Kelly was trying unsuccessfully to corner the detective. I did a quick pan of the gathering crowd, making sure to include the glaring yellow tapes as well as the flashing lights of the police cars.

Kelly was getting anxious. It was almost four. John had called and said that we were going to be headlining the live broadcast at six. We drove to the police station, where we managed to get some good shots of the suspect as he was transported to a holding cell. His name, we were told, was Hector Gonzalez; Hispanic, forty-five, with no prior record. As of yet, the police had no motive for the stabbing. Hector looked dazed and confused as he walked past us. The reporters shouted questions at him, but he ignored them. I watched him go by, thinking that he did not have the look of a man who had just ushered three souls into eternity. Then again, they never do.

As soon as he was out of sight, I got us set up in front of the courthouse for Kelly's live report. Then Kelly recorded her voiceover and I hunkered down inside the van and got to work slapping together my footage, matching her words to my video. I finished with minutes to spare and uploaded the edited piece to the WFAC server. We had about a minute to catch our breath and then we went live.

I'll give her credit. Kelly did a bang-up job. Her delivery was crisp and professional, and the copy she had written was fast paced and concise. I had a feeling that, if she could keep her wits about her, she would go far in the business.

Once we were done, Kelly helped me tear down. We loaded up the van and headed to the station. Kelly was flushed with the excitement of having just done a live report and jabbered all the way back. When we arrived at WFAC, she checked the board for her next assignment while I commandeered Edit Bay Two. A follow up report would air at noon, with another in the 6 p.m. broadcast. Now that I had the time, I wanted to add a few flourishes to the video and tighten things up a bit. Kelly was assigned to do a background check on Hector Gonzalez. We set a time for her to come in and record an updated voiceover and then got busy on our respective tasks.

Barriers

I had not been able to work the shot of the painting into my first cut and wanted to add it to the update. I thought it would make a strong statement; a portrait of humanity getting evicted from paradise, overlooking a murder scene. The only thing was, I couldn't make it fit. There was simply no place to slip it in. I sat there in that small room, staring at the screen. There were Adam and Eve, naked except for a few wisps of strategically placed clothing. There was the angel, stern yet somehow effeminate, wielding a blazing sword. There was Eden...

I'm not big on paintings, particularly religious ones, but for some reason, this one moved me. The longer I stared at it, the more real it seemed. I kept looking over the angel's shoulder, trying to peer further and further into the background. For a few eternal seconds, I was absolutely sure that, if I reached out, my hand would pass through the screen and I would be able to touch paradise. A desperate, overwhelming sense of longing washed through me. Look, I don't know how we got here, whether we were born out of the mind of God or climbed down from a tree. I've certainly never believed in a literal Garden of Eden, but as I sat there, I found myself wishing with every fiber of my being that I could step into that painting, slip past the angel and claim my place in paradise.

Left alone, I still might be sitting there, but John banged on the door and told me to stop hogging the edit bay. I shoved my feelings aside and tried to concentrate. I finally gave up on the painting and added a few extra shots of the sanctuary instead. The last insert was my pan of the church exterior. I was just about to wrap things up when something caught my eye. Even at that hour, some of the local night dwellers had been loitering around the parameter. I hadn't noticed then, but one of the spectators was dressed as a priest. This caught me by surprise. Was he a part of this particular parish? Did he know the victims?

There had not been a lot of light, but my camera boasted incredible resolution. I could easily make out his face. He was young, probably in his early twenties, with a lean build and dark, close cropped black hair. I wondered if he was an intern or trainee or whatever you call junior priests. He was standing there, just outside the police line, looking toward the church entrance.

Don't ask me how I knew, but the more I stared at him, the more I was certain that he was somehow connected to the murders. Had the police questioned him? Of course they had, I assured myself. Our cops were a pretty good lot, and if there had been even a hint of something suspicious, this same priest would now be sitting in a small room, undergoing questioning by three or four cranky detectives. And yet...

There was something wrong. Video doesn't lie. Our eyes might deceive us, or our brains might rationalize something away, but video, particularly raw footage, is stark reality. I ran the footage back to the beginning of the pan and played it again. The longing I felt over the painting had disappeared and was replaced by a growing sense of dread. Something was there; something that I could not see with my eyes but could feel with my...*soul* is the only word I can think of. I centered the shot on the priest and froze it. My eyes locked with his and I could not look away. I suddenly felt as if I was trying to wade through waist deep tar. My breathing slowed and my eyes drooped. *Who are*

Barriers

you? I asked silently.

We are your bondage.

I jerked back in my chair, startled. The voice in my head was my own, but I had absolutely no idea where that thought had come from. I realized that I must have dozed off. My mind was dredging up the night's events and trying to turn them into some kind of nightmare. Not surprising, really. I looked at the freeze frame of the priest.

His eyes were glowing.

I let out a yelp, bolted out of my chair and through the door. The hall was filled with people rushing back and forth, preparing for the next broadcast. No one paid any attention to me and after a few moments, I was able to get myself together. I stepped back into the bay.

The priest's eyes were still glowing. I reached over and shut off the dim track lights that ran overhead. Darkness filled the edit bay, with only the glowing computer screen providing any light. The glow went out of the priest's eyes, leaving them shrouded in darkness far deeper than the bay.

I tried to feel relieved. I was awake, sober and rational. What I had seen was impossible. People's eyes do not glow, especially when they are only images on a screen. It was just the reflection of the track lights.

But I was wrong and I knew it. Rather, I could feel it. I stared at the screen, looking deep into the priest's now dark eyes and I felt something else.

He was *seeing* me.

I wanted to scream. I *needed* to scream. I tried to open my mouth, but my jaw would not cooperate. Something had me, something that I could not even begin to describe or resist...something old, powerful and malevolent.

Gathering what little resolve I could, I stepped over to the computer. I uploaded the revised piece and got out of the freeze frame. The priest disappeared, not that it mattered. I told John that the piece was finished and walked out of the building. No one saw me leave, but sooner or later John would be screaming bloody murder. I still had several assignments on the board, but I didn't care. I had to go back to the crime scene. This was not a matter of choice. I didn't want to face my fears or unravel the Mystery Of The Priest With The Glowing Eyes. I had no say in the matter. I was being dragged back and there was nothing that I could do to resist.

It was just after 7 a.m. when I got to the church. The sky was beginning to get that almost-there gray tint that heralds the arrival of morning. The police tape was still in place, but the squad cars were gone. All of the cars were gone, in fact, which was unusual. Forensics should still have been busy, and at least one uniformed officer would have pulled guard duty. I parked across the street and got out of my car.

The church doors were unlocked. I pushed them open and went inside. The lights were on but no one was in sight. The two blood-written phrases had been cleaned away, but the dark, almost black stains still defiled the carpet. I walked down the center aisle and stopped in front of the painting. I took a moment to study it, but unlike the video, it seemed pale and cheap…flat.

"You know what I've always hated about the Catholic Church?" The voice came from my left. I whirled, heart pounding, but I already knew who would be there. The young priest was standing in front of the altar, arms folded across his chest. "They've got hundreds of millions of dollars of rare and invaluable artwork in Rome, not to mention other major cities, but most of the local parishes get stuck with crap like that. Go figure." He unfolded his arms and, with a fluid grace that was disturbingly inhuman, crossed the sanctuary. He stopped a few feet away, his dark eyes glinting cruelly in the dim light.

I could not move. I could not speak, and even breathing was becoming difficult. This...man...held me in a way that allowed for no resistance. My will was completely subjugated. I had no control over my body or my mind. He knew it too. Beneath that casual demeanor, I could feel him gloating.

"Really though," he continued, "one religion is as bad as the next. Most of them promise some kind of blissful afterlife...streets of gold, willing virgins, whatever...and they're all so wrong. Don't you agree?" His face had changed as he spoke. His eyes, those hateful, empty eyes, had grown to almost twice their normal size. There were no whites, only two black bottomless pits. He nodded toward the painting. "Face it," he said. I obeyed without hesitation. A second later, I heard a harsh click and suddenly a knife floated in front of my eyes. "They died by this blade," whispered the priest, his lips now touching my ear. "They died because they saw...because they dared hope. Maybe now it's your turn. Or maybe I can place the blame for their deaths on you, like I did poor Hector. What do you think?" A single tear squirted out of my left eye. If I could, I would have screamed myself hoarse. I've seen a lot of bad stuff in the course of my career, but for the first time in my life, I had come face to face with something that was wholly, unabashedly, *proudly* evil...something that had dug its claws deep into my soul. The knife lowered and I felt its scalpel-sharp edge press against my throat. "Why don't you kneel down," he said, and again I obeyed. The priest laid a warm, heavy hand on the top of my head, as if giving some kind of perverse blessing.

"You saw something on your recording," he said. It was not a question. "Not me, but before, when you were looking at the painting. Something you weren't supposed to see. I know. *We* always know. It happens more often than you would think, especially in this damned digital age. High-definition cameras are getting better and seeing more than they should." Suddenly he gripped the top of my head and twisted it until I was looking up at him. "Isn't there something that you would like to ask me?" I felt my tongue loosen.

"Who...are...you?" I could barely whisper. He smiled down at me.

"I'm the good shepherd," he answered, and laughed. I could hear the scream of a thousand damned souls in that laugh. "Or not. If you must know, we call ourselves the Clergy...sometimes." He laughed again and twisted my head back to face the painting. "I'm the guy who herds you poor souls into the afterlife." He knelt in front of me. "I'm going to show you something, and then...well, we'll see." He reached into his jacket pocket and pulled out a sturdy looking gold necklace. It glittered coldly as he held it up before my eyes. "Pay attention now," he said and slipped it over my head. As soon as it fell around my neck, he twisted it hard. The tiny links bit deep into my skin. I could feel

Barriers

my windpipe constricting. I started to gasp, trying to force in the air, but his grip was too tight. The more I heaved, the harder he squeezed. The world began to fade.

"Look at the painting, Kurt," he commanded, and I struggled to obey. It seemed impossibly far away. I knew that I had scant seconds of life left. *I'm being murdered.* That single thought chased its tale inside my dying mind. *Oh God, I'm being murdered in a church.*

And then.

I saw it. I don't know whether I died, or came so close as to make no difference, but I saw it. I saw what he wanted me to see, what has haunted my every thought and dream since that morning.

Without any hint of transition, the painting changed. Suddenly I wasn't looking at a cheap reproduction hanging on a bare wall. It became a doorway; a doorway into a place so fantastic that my mind could not accept its existence. Every lost hope, every desperate dream of paradise, every desire of peace, joy and love was there in front of me. I saw a place where there was no hate or war; a place where priests did not murder people in churches. *I saw heaven.*

It was a single, perfect moment.

My soul screamed in agony, not because of my glimpse into paradise, but because of who was guarding it. The angel was still there, only now he was no longer gentle and effeminate. His eyes were aflame, his hair was snow white, and his face was stern and unyielding. He held his sword ready, and I knew that to challenge him would mean not only the death of my body, but the death of my soul. He held his hand up in a gesture of ultimate rejection, and I knew at that moment that I was damned.

Without warning the vision disappeared and I found myself lying face down on the floor. The chain was gone and I could breathe again. I gulped in the air with the desperation of a drowning man. It took a long time to get my body back under control, but the priest was patient. *We are patient.* I opened my eyes and saw the toes of his black shoes just inches from my face.

"Do you understand now?" he asked in that smug, assured voice. I started to sob. "I'll take that as a yes," he said, satisfied. "Go on. I'll call when I want you. You'll come, of course." I couldn't speak, but he knew that I would obey. I had been tagged...branded. He turned and walked away as I scrambled to my feet and staggered out of the church.

I never went back to WFAC, never even called to let them know I was quitting. I settled my affairs as fast as I could, handed the bulk of my property over to my ex, and left Tampa forever.

That was three weeks ago. Right now, I'm typing this on my old laptop, sitting in a tiny diner somewhere deep in the heart of Kentucky. I've got enough money to last maybe another month or so. After that, well, like the priest said, we'll see. As soon as I finish, I'm going to send this little tale to a friend. I don't expect that he'll believe a word of it, but he has a connection or two in the publishing industry. If he can sell it as fiction to a decent market, my kids will get a few extra things for their birthdays. If he can't, well, it doesn't really matter. Nothing really matters, except living. I don't want to die. Let me repeat that.

I don't want to die.

I've never been religious, but I know that a lot of

Barriers

folks believe that we are poised between heaven and hell, with the choice between the two being ours. The bottom line is a sense of hope...that there is something better waiting for us after this life is over. As I gazed into that incredible painting, the life being choked out of me by a creature masquerading as a priest, I understood.

They're wrong. They're all wrong. That angel wasn't just there for me. He was there for all of us. The door to paradise is closed. Whatever awaits us after this life is...not nice. Call it cruel, call it unfair, or call it what it probably is - entropy of the soul. We are all damned. The damned are us. *The damned are here*.

Why was I allowed to see? I don't really know, but understand this. That priest has friends, and whatever they are...shepherds to the afterlife, the Clergy, whatever...they're cruel, and I've got a hunch that they're everywhere. Their purpose may be to herd us into the afterlife, but they enjoy inflicting pain along the way. Maybe my particular Clergyman was just bored and needed a new plaything. When he gets tired of me, he'll call me in. I'll go of course, and he'll usher me down to whatever horrors are waiting.

Except...

I keep thinking back to what he said about his three victims as he held his knife to my throat. *They died because they saw... because they dared hope.* Hope for what? There's only one answer to that - salvation.

What if there's a way? What if there's a way to sneak past that angel? What if I can find a way into paradise?

What if heaven has a back door?

A fool's hope? Maybe, but it's all I've got.

David F. Gray

So I keep moving. My time is short. I can feel him watching me. Sooner or later, he'll call me in, but until then, I've got to keep looking. Maybe I'll get lucky. Maybe the Clergy are not the only guides into the afterlife. Maybe I'll find the way home.

God, please let me find the way home.

The Cypress Wood Terror

The masked serial killer grabbed the lovely, half naked blonde from behind and jammed the serrated blade of the hunting knife deep into her back. The blood spewed from her mouth in an arc that covered at least five feet, splattering her stunned boyfriend from waist to shoulders.

I rubbed my eyes and groaned. While I had to give the director credit for chancing a practical gag over CGI, he really should have known better. The overall effect was cheesy at best and embarrassing at worst.

Fortunately, I was there to save the day.

I glanced at my watch and saw that it was a few minutes past midnight. A few years back, this would have been normal for me. I preferred working through the night. Fewer people meant fewer interruptions. More often than not I would walk out of Cypress Wood Studios well past daylight, go home, crash, come back late in the afternoon and do it all over again.

Of course, at the time I had been single, carefree, and making way too much money. Cypress Wood may have been a smaller production house by Hollywood standards, but it maintained a healthy, well-funded clientele, and the owners were happy to share that wealth. I ran with a small group of friends who worked hard and played harder, oblivious to the fact that life changes.

For me, Jenny Mallon was that change. She started working at Cypress Wood a little over six years ago as an assistant editor. She was twenty-one, fresh out of film school, and eager to prove herself. She was also a

David F. Gray

stunning beauty. Barely five feet in height, she sported blonde hair that, unlike the unfortunate co-ed on my left screen, did not come out of a bottle. She was petite and perfectly proportioned, and I fell in love with her the instant I laid eyes on her.

I had competition, namely every single man (and two women) on the Cypress Wood staff. She made a pretense of playing the field, but it was mostly for show. We hit it off immediately. Don't ask me why, but she fell for me as hard as I did for her. We were married less than a year after we started dating. Five years later we were still going strong.

Jenny discovered that she preferred production to postproduction and about a year after we were married managed to get hired as production assistant on a low budget indie flick. It was a modest hit and since the director liked surrounding himself with the same people from picture to picture, she was now firmly entrenched as his executive assistant. I was happy at Cypress Wood, she was happy shooting movies, and we were both happy with each other. We were making serious money and life was just about as good as it could get.

I froze the image of the hapless coed on the screen and picked up the shooting script, complete with the director's notes. That director, DeVonte Edwards, had already turned in his cut, so as far as the producers were concerned, his job was done. It was now my job to take his two hour and twenty-minute opus and slash it down to a petite running time of one hour and forty-five minutes.

I had worked with the producers on two other features, so they trusted me to do what needed to be done. That meant I was alone in Edit Bay Three, and

Barriers

that suited me just fine. It was the smallest bay at Cypress Wood, maybe fifteen feet square and lit with five dim track lights set into the tiled ceiling. I sat at a wide desk that held two thirty-inch screens, a keyboard, a mouse and a stylus. On the gray carpeted wall in front of the desk, about six feet away, was an ultra-high-definition eighty-inch screen flanked by two large, high-end speakers. Two identical speakers hung on the wall behind me and one on each wall to my left and right. The amplifiers were rack-mounted under the desk. EB-3 was soundproofed, which meant I could crank up the volume without disturbing anyone else who might be working late. All of the raw footage had been dumped onto one of Cypress Wood's many servers and was easily accessible. I had all the tools I needed at my fingertips.

I thumbed through the script until I found the scene that matched the one on my screen and chuckled when I read DeVonte's notes. They were simple and to the point. *Dean, for the love of God, save me!* I laid the script on the wide desk, slid the frozen scene over to my right screen, and got to work.

Four hours later, I sat back and played the entire scene from start to finish on the big screen. I had chopped almost two minutes out of it, paring it down to a lean three minutes and ten seconds. That was the easy part. Making all that fake blood disappear was much harder and far more time consuming. I had managed to get rid of the worst of it with a few well-placed cuts. The rest I replaced with millions of tiny, computer-generated droplets of equally fake blood. True, I had never seen anyone stabbed, but the overall effect looked much more realistic. I still had at least another two days' worth of work to do on that scene, and at least three more weeks before I would hand in the finished product, but I was comfortably ahead of schedule. That should translate into a healthy bonus, and I was already envisioning a long weekend in the mountains with Jenny.

"That's good work." I jumped in my chair and swiveled to face the door. I had been so engrossed with my work that I had not heard it open. Ron Wibley, one of my counterparts, stood there, leaning against the frame and holding a cup of steaming coffee in a blue Cypress Wood mug. He knew better than to step into the bay. 'No food or beverages in technical areas' was a hard and fast rule that meant instant dismissal if broken. Liquid and electronics do not mix. Ron saw that he had startled me and waved his free hand in apology. "Sorry," he said.

"No problem," I replied. "In fact, I wouldn't mind a fresh set of eyes." Ron nodded and I played the scene again.

We got along okay, Ron and I...not great, but okay. He had been at Cypress Wood a few years longer than me, and thus had seniority. He was a good editor, but the simple fact was, I was better. He had also been one of Jenny's suitors. It tended to make things awkward between us. He never admitted it...to me at least...but I think he had fallen for her as hard as I did. She had let him down as gently as she could, but I'm pretty sure the rejection had devastated him.

Physically he was fairly ordinary...maybe two or three inches shorter than me, with limp dark brown hair and a build that was at present stocky but in a few years would probably translate to heavy. He wore thick, horn-rimmed glassed that magnified his brown eyes just enough to give him a slightly creepy look. Still, he was nice enough. He even came to our wedding and when he wished us all the best, he seemed to mean it.

"I think you got it," he said when the scene ended. "You might consider trimming another few frames off that reaction shot, but once you clean up the rest of that blood, you're good."

"Thanks," I said. "That helps a lot. What are you working on?"

"That Honda commercial," said Ron. "You know, all the green screen stuff?" I nodded. Honda retained a much larger agency, but a series of unfortunate events had forced them to farm out some of the work to smaller houses like Cypress Wood. It was an amazing opportunity. If they liked us, it would mean a lot more work and a lot more money. Did I say that I was a better editor than Ron? Maybe, but when it came to commercials, the man was a genius.

"I'm just finishing up the first cut," said Ron. "When you get a moment, maybe you could return the favor and give me a fresh set of eyes."

"Sure," I said. "Where are you?"

"A Control," said Ron. He saw my look of surprise and shrugged. A Control was a control room designed for live production. It could be used for editing, of course, but only when it wasn't being used for studio work. "The links to the servers for Bay One and Two went down a few hours ago, so I moved," he said. "The tech guys say they have to overnight a bunch of new modules, so they won't be back up until sometime late tomorrow morning."

"Got it," I said. I arched my back and raised both

arms in a long stretch. "What else is going on?"

"Nothing," said Ron. "Other than you and me, it's just Billy in security and he's manning the front desk. Carl left about an hour ago. Said there's nothing he could do until those modules get here." I frowned at that. Carl was our chief engineer, and Cypress Wood was his baby. He was highly protective of each piece of equipment. For him to leave when something was offline, even when there was nothing he could do about it, was unusual. The man was obsessive. I shook off a sudden sense of unease and nodded.

"Give me twenty minutes," I said. "I'll wander over as soon as I make a few notes." Ron nodded and left, closing the door behind him. It took a little longer than twenty minutes, but finally I felt satisfied enough to take a short break. I made doubly sure that all my work was backed up and headed over to A Control.

Cypress Wood Studios is a full-service production facility. We have two large studios equipped with ten top-of-the-line HD cameras. There are two control rooms, 'A' and 'B', as well as three state-of-the-art edit bays. The entire facility is housed in a converted rectangular warehouse. In the back is the prop room along with shipping and receiving. Studios A and B are parallel to each other, separated by a wide hall we call the Air Lock. Halls also run along the outer wall of each studio. Both halls and Air Lock end with a set of heavy double doors that lead directly into another hall that surrounds the entire the technical area. These doors are secured with high-end locks that require both a card and a combination to open.

The technical area is laid out in a large square. The edit bays line the west side, while access to the two

Barriers

control rooms is from a hall on the east. The north side houses engineering as well as access to the servers. The south side, the side facing the studios, is a solid wall. It's a good arrangement. There's enough sound proofing and separation so that every area can be busy without anyone getting in anyone else's way.

I took my time walking down the north hall. I was stiff and my back was sore, so I tried to stretch as I walked. I passed the wide double doors on my right that led to the lobby, giving them a tug just to make sure they were locked. A few feet further allowed me to peek through the window into engineering on my left. It was an impressive room. The opposite wall boasted two ninety-inch screens that could be divided into sectors as small as six inches and programmed to access any camera or the output of any bay or control room in the building. On the left and right were banks of instruments that not only monitored Cypress Wood's delicate systems but could be used to access any network on any satellite.

I continued on to the end of the hall, hung a left, went another ten feet to the entrance to A Control. I peeked through the waist high window set into the door, but Ron was nowhere in sight. I shrugged and stepped inside.

While not as large as engineering, A Control was just as impressive. Facing me were two eighty-inch screens that could be partitioned into smaller areas to show the outputs of any or all of our cameras, as well as feeds from the servers. In the center of the left screen a large, forty-inch sector was set aside for 'Preview', while an identical sector on the right screen was designated 'Program'. The 'Program' sector featured a beauty shot of one of Honda's latest models and the 'Preview' sector held a pair of actors standing in front of the large green screen that dominated one corner of Studio B.

A fifteen-foot-long control panel sat in the middle of A Control and boasted one of the best production switchers on the market. To the right of the switcher was an equally impressive audio board, and to the left sat a powerful graphics unit. Next to the graphics unit was a smaller screen, and in front of that were ten rectangular control units that could be delegated to monitor the studio cameras. A smaller producer's desk sat about six feet behind the main control panel. At the moment it held a keyboard along with two thirty-inch screens…the editing system Ron was using.

I figured that Ron had probably taken a potty break, so I sat down in one of the two chairs in front of the editor and waited. I could have played the commercial myself, but that would have been inconsiderate. Instead, I leaned back in the chair and tried to relax. The low lighting, the cool air and the comfortable chair all conspired to lead me into a light doze.

On the right program screen, the Honda flickered. I blinked, wondering if I had imagined it. It flickered again, and an instant later the entire sector went black. I groaned and sat up. If a server was crashing or another module was going bad, we were going to be in real trouble...as in missed deadlines, lost clients and no bonuses trouble. I started to get up and head back to EB-3 but suddenly the screen flared to life, only now, instead of the Honda, I could see Studio B, complete with green screen, staring back at me.

It took me a few seconds to understand that what I

Barriers

was seeing was impossible. The screens in A Control could only be programmed from the production switcher in front of me. There was no way that anyone could switch sources remotely, not even in engineering. I was still trying to process this when the Preview sector on the left blinked and went to black. When it came back up, it was showing a wide shot of Studio A.

"What the..." I slid out of my chair and stepped over to the production switcher. As I did, there was another flash and ten new, smaller squares appeared running along the bottom of both screens, five on each. I punched a few buttons on the switcher but it seemed to have crashed. The ten smaller squares flashed again, and now they each held a view from one of our studio cameras. Each camera was labeled with a number...cam 1, cam 2, cam 3 and so on. Cameras 1 through 5 were in Studio A, while 6 through 10 were in B. "No way," I muttered, still punching buttons. Only the fluorescents were on in both studios. The video wasn't all that bright, but I could still see the various sets.

My first thought was that Ron was pulling some kind of stunt. With everyone else except for Billy gone, he was the only one with the technical savvy to pull it off, but I kept coming back to the simple fact that the screens could not be remotely programmed. I stared at them for another second or two and then decided to go over to engineering. It was possible that Carl or one of the other engineers had rewritten the software so that the screens could be accessed from there. Maybe...

On the left screen, the shot labeled Cam 1 started moving. I watched as it slid past an interview set that was scheduled to be torn down at the end of the week. A faux news set that was being used to tape an infomercial came into view and then disappeared just as quickly. The camera view swiveled right and started trucking along the outer hall toward the door that led to the technical area. I barely processed this when Cam 2 started to move, following Cam 1 past the two sets and toward the same door.

I had been feeling uneasy since my conversation with Ron, but now, as I stared at the moving cameras, that unease morphed into real fear. I stared at the shot on Cam 2. It was following close behind Cam 1, so I should have seen the camera, the dolly and whoever was pushing it, but all I could see was the door to the technical area. There was no camera, no dolly and no operator.

An instant later the rest of the camera shots started to move. Cams 3, 4 and 5 left Studio A and started trucking down the Air Lock toward the central entrance to the tech area. Cams 6 & 7 were heading through Studio B toward the opposite wall and the third entrance. 8, 9 and 10 seemed to be combing through the prop area. I could not see a single camera in any of the shots.

I was still trying to convince myself that I was the victim of some elaborate joke, but as I watched, Cam 1 reached the first set of doors to the technical area. It stopped for a moment and then tilted down to study the security lock bolted on the wall to the right. The lock consisted of a numerical keypad and a sensor that read our identity cards. On the top was a digital display. Cam 1 zoomed into a tight shot of the keypad and a moment later, I could see the buttons move. The display read the numbers as they were punched. It was a five-digit sequence, and the instant the last number

Barriers

was entered the doors opened. The hall separating the tech area from the studios came into view. The shot panned right and started moving again. Seconds later Cam 2's shot followed Cam 1 into the hall.

I took a step back, fully intending to get out of A Control, but I could not tear my eyes from the screens. Cams 3 and 4 reached the doors at the end of the Air Lock. The sequence was repeated, much faster this time, and the camera shots passed through the open doors and turned right. An instant later Cams 5, 6 and 7 passed through the final set of doors. Cams 1 & 2 were now moving straight toward A Control, while Cams 3 and 4 were gliding past Edit Bay 3. When Cam 3 reached the door, it panned left. The bay came into view. I could see the final frame of the scene I had been working on displayed on the main screen, just as I had left it. The shot hovered there for a moment and then continued down the hall.

I suddenly realized that I was about to be surrounded. Never mind that what I was seeing was impossible to the point of absurdity. In a matter of minutes, the shots on Cams 1 through 7 would have me effectively trapped in A Control.

I realized something else. I needed to get out of the building...fast. I could not begin to imagine what force or intelligence was manipulating those shots, but I was absolutely certain that I did not want to find out. I backed away from the console, keeping my eyes on the screens. Again the screen flickered, and now Cams 1 and 2 were displayed on the Preview and Program sectors.

I stumbled backward, but just as I made it to the door, Cam 1's shot swung around, revealing the hall that led directly to A Control. I could easily see the other side of the door that I was about to walk through. There was no other way out. Suppressing a whimper, I slid to the floor and pressed hard against the door.

I could still see Cam 1's shot on the Preview sector, and as I watched, it drew even with the door. It hovered there for a second and then panned right. A Control slid into view. The shot hesitated and then zoomed into the switcher. It moved across the multicolored buttons and then zoomed out again, panning left until it was shooting straight through the door. Then it began to tilt down, drawing closer and closer to where I was crouching. I was trapped, but inches before my right foot would have been revealed, the shot stopped moving. It hovered there for several seconds, as if uncertain. Then it tilted up and panned the control room again.

The door shuddered, as if something very large and heavy leaned against it. I could feel it start to give way. The handle rattled and the frame creaked. I had a vision of the door shattering into thousands of tiny shards of wood and glass, shredding me in the process. A part of me actually welcomed the idea. I had a strong feeling that being flayed by an exploding door was infinitely better than being caught by the force responsible for the shattering.

The creaking stopped. The shot on the screens swung left, back to the hall and continued forward. When it reached the corner, it turned and headed toward Edit Bay 3. I stared at the screen, waiting for another view of A Control to appear, but for the moment, the hall outside was clear. I scrambled to my feet and staggered over to the switcher.

Barriers

The camera shots were still active, but all of them were now on the other side of the technical area, blocking the entrance to the lobby. For the moment, a single path to the studios and prop room was clear.

I bolted through the door and ran down the hall to the entrance to Studio A. My only thought was to get out of the building, get to my car and get back to Jenny. I could use the loading dock that was just past the prop room. It meant setting off the alarm but that was the least of my worries. My hands were shaking, but I managed to punch in my security code. I started to pull the door open but sensed movement to my left. I glanced down the hall.

The next thing I remember I was running and screaming through the prop room to the loading dock. I have no memory of going through the door or running through Studio A. I also have no memory of what I may have seen or not seen coming toward me in that hall. I count that as a mercy, because I think that if I ever do remember, I will go insane.

The loading dock consisted of a large, wide entrance shuttered by a sturdy metal door that rolled down and locked in place. Next to that was a standard sized door that, although locked, opened easily from the inside. Outside was a retention ditch that bordered a wide field.

Just before I reached the door, something began to pound on it from the outside. At the same time the metal door covering the shipping entrance began to shudder. I pulled up, choking down a scream. Behind me I heard the double doors to the Airlock open.

There was nowhere to go, and I suddenly realized that the opening I had been given in A Control was no accident. I was in the prop room because that was where *they* wanted me. I started to back away from the loading dock, thinking that maybe there might be a place to hide among all the props, but before I could turn I was hit from behind. My vision exploded into millions of tiny, blazing points of light. I fell forward and hit the cold cement floor hard. I felt hands grab my feet and start to drag me across the floor. Then, like the end of so many movies I had edited, my mind faded to black.

* * *

I groaned as I fought my way back to consciousness. My head was on fire and my nose was throbbing. I could feel something wet trickling out of it. I reached up to grab my head and the instant I touched my face my memory returned. My eyes snapped open and I sat up. My stomach heaved and I nearly lost my last meal, but a couple of deep breaths helped the nausea subside.

I was sitting on a couch in Studio B, on one of the generic interview sets we kept on hand. Directly in front of me were cameras six through ten. I nearly screamed I until saw that they were powered down and locked in place, exactly where they had been when I had reported for work.

I looked to my left and this time I did scream. Carl was there, sitting behind the interviewer's desk. At least, I think it was Carl. The body had the right build, and I could see his employee security card clamped to his shirt pocket. That was where any similarities to the man I had known for years ended. The lower half of his body was missing, as was his head. The torso, complete with Carl's hairy arms, had been shoved into the chair

Barriers

like a child's broken doll and propped up by some of the cushions from the couch. There was blood everywhere, and I could see bits of his insides radiating out from the bottom of his torso like the roots of some obscene plant. I screamed again and rolled off the couch, landing on all fours.

"I didn't want him to suffer, but they like to play." The voice came from my right. I looked and saw Ron standing next to an announcer's podium, staring at me through those thick glasses.

"Ron?" It was all I could manage. My throat was dry and the instant I said his name I started to cough.

"He was in the way. If he had just left like he was supposed to, he would still be alive." Ron stepped around the podium and moved to the edge of the set, just a few feet away. "*You*, on the other hand," he snarled, "I want you to hurt...a *lot*. You took Jenny from me. I loved her and you took her from me." Somehow I got my cough under control.

"Ron? What..."

"I made a deal," said Ron. He smiled and shook his head. "Not really. You don't make deals with *them*. You give them what they want, and if that makes them happy, then they might give you a little something in return. Scraps from the table, so to speak." He looked across the studio to the large green screen that dominated the entire north side. "I gave them a way in, and Jenny is my scrap. They're going to give her to me." My head was on fire and my thoughts were incoherent, but when Ron mentioned my wife, my adrenalin surged and my mind cleared. I focused on him, thinking of those floating shots that had herded me into the prop room.

"What have you done?" I said in a low voice. "And who the hell are they?" Ron's smile became a wide, cruel grin. The bastard actually laughed.

"They're old...beyond old, really, maybe older than the universe itself," he said. "But they've only recently become aware of us." He pointed to the row of cameras beside him. "It's the high-definition tech," he said. "We're constantly trying to figure out ways to make our pictures clearer, brighter, and more vivid." He shrugged. "I think that coupled with all the Wi-Fi, smart phones and other wireless tech, somehow our big, bright pictures became windows into our reality. They found those windows and turned them into doors."

"What, like something out of *Poltergeist*?" I gasped. "That's...insane."

"Maybe," he said. "But I don't think they use the signal. I think that they *are* the signal. When humanity first started using radio waves, we were somehow accessing the lowest part of their unconscious mind, but when we developed hi def and Wi-Fi, we invaded their conscious thoughts. They're just returning the favor." He laughed again.

"If you stare at those screens long enough, they start to reach out to you, and not just places like Cypress Wood. Any HD TV or monitor is a portal for them." He pointed at my pants pocket. "They can even use that fancy new iPhone you're so proud of." He looked down and for just an instant, I saw a look of pure terror cross his face.

"They found me," he said in a low voice. "And they *talked* to me. They told me that they can influence our thoughts. I get the feeling that a lot of people have seen them but have been made to forget." Behind him the

Barriers

green screen started to ripple and bulge. Whatever had herded me was behind it. In seconds, it would either be coming through it or around it. Ron started to back away.

"But I don't care about any of that," he said. "What I do know is that they like to...play...with us." He nodded at Carl's body. "You're next. Then they'll go to work on Jenny. They won't harm her body, just adjust her mind a little. In a few months, she'll have forgotten you and be in love with me. I could have just let them take you, but I wanted you to know, when you're slowly being ripped apart, that I'm going to have Jenny. I wanted..."

I sprang to my feet and charged. I took real satisfaction in wiping that smug look off his face as I ploughed into him. I wanted to beat the bastard to a pulp, but I wanted to get out of the building and back to my wife even more. I lowered my shoulders and hit him hard, grabbing him around his waist. He started to yell but I knocked the wind out of him. My legs kept churning and I forced him across the studio to the shuddering, bulging green screen.

My mind had cleared enough so that I understood two vital facts. One, whatever or whoever Ron was playing with, they were subject to physical barriers. They had been forced to open the doors to the technical area rather than just going through them. Two...

They liked to play.

And I had a feeling that they really didn't care with whom they played.

Desperation gave me the advantage. I could see the green screen fraying. More importantly, I could feel them leaking around the edges of screen, sloughing into Studio B like some kind of foul blob.

David F. Gray

Now it was Ron's turn to scream. His feet scrambled against the concrete, but with a final, desperate surge, I shoved him through the green screen. It fluttered and ripped from top to bottom. Ron screamed again as he fell through the rip. He tried to pull back, but something grabbed him from the other side. I turned away as his scream became a high-pitched wail. Whatever had him, I did *not* want to see it.

I stumbled across the studio, praying that the way was clear. Behind me, Ron's screams grew louder and then abruptly stopped. Seconds later they were replaced by high-pitched, insane laughter. That laughter chased me as I ran through the prop room and the loading dock. I hit the door at full speed, the impact nearly dislocating my shoulder, and threw it open. The alarm sounded but I barely noticed.

I half expected to be devoured by some nameless horror once I got outside, but the only thing that greeted me as I stumbled through the door was the early morning sunlight. I ran around the building, got into my car and peeled out of the parking lot. As soon as I hit the main highway, I yanked my phone out of my pocket and threw it out of the window.

Twenty minutes later, I pulled into the driveway of the house Jenny and I had bought less than a year ago. The instant my feet hit the pavement, the front door opened and Jenny rushed out. I groaned in relief and grabbed her in a fierce hug. She fell into my arms, sobbing.

"I've been trying to call you for hours," she gasped, clinging to me as tightly as I was clinging to her. "Your phone kept going to voice mail." I pulled away and saw that she was trembling. I ignored the first five questions

Barriers

that ran through my mind and instead said the only thing that mattered.

"Get a bag packed," I said. "We're leaving." She stared at me for a few seconds. Then she asked me a short, simple question...a question that has haunted me every second of every day since.

"Is this about Ron?" I jerked back, as if she had slapped me.

"How did you..."

"Oh God," she sobbed. "I knew it!"

"Jenny?"

"I've been dreaming about him all night," said Jenny. "He came to me and said he killed you and that I belonged to him."

"It's okay," I lied.

"He takes me away and what he does to me..." She wrapped her arms around my waist held me tight. "But that's not the worst part. Dean, part of me wants to go with him. Do you understand? I *want* to go. What's happening to me?" I went cold inside.

"Just get packed," I said. "We're getting out of town and I don't think we're coming back."

* * *

That was six months ago. Police, responding to the alarm, found Carl's body in Studio B. They searched the rest of the building and discovered what was left of Billy, the security guard, stuffed between the servers. When they searched A Control, they found a video waiting for them on both screens. In it, Ron took credit for the murders. The fact that he was cradling Carl's head in one arm convinced the police that he was telling the truth. Ron had already uploaded the video to YouTube, and within hours it had gone viral.

A statewide manhunt was instituted, not only for him but for me and Jenny. When they could not find me at Cypress Wood, they searched our home. They were not sure if we were accomplices or victims, but they wanted to talk to us. I would have gladly told them everything, but I had a bad feeling that Ron, or rather the thing he had become, would be hunting us. The last thing I wanted was to be stuck for hours at the local police station.

Jenny and I drove out of Los Angeles on Interstate 10, but as soon as we could we switched to the state routes. I made a single stop at our bank and emptied our savings account. It was risky, but we managed to get our money and get out of town.

For the past six months, we have kept moving. We left Jenny's phone and our pads at our house. I even disconnected the satellite radio and GPS in our Range Rover. Our latest stop is a cheap motel in a little Texan town. We have enough money to last another few months, but as of this morning, it doesn't matter.

Ron is following us. I can tell because wherever he stops, he kills. His body count is beyond staggering...seven towns and twenty-seven bodies...and every town is one where we have stayed. No matter how fast or far we travel, he's always behind us, and he's gaining ground. The statewide manhunt has become nationwide, but he always manages to escape the dragnets.

That's not the worst part. Jenny has become increasingly distant. I can feel her slipping away. They got into her mind and they won't let go. This morning,

Barriers

when I woke up, she was gone. I ran outside and saw that she had taken the Range Rover. I have no doubt that, even as I write this, she is with Ron, and the images that are playing themselves out in my mind are driving me to the edge of sanity.

I've got nowhere to go, and it really doesn't matter. I'm a loose end. Whatever is inside Ron won't let me live, which means that sooner or later they're going to come for me. So I'm going to stay right here and wait. Maybe there's still enough of Jenny's mind left to let me win her back, but I keep coming back to that one damnable thing Ron said about them.

They like to play.

* * *

To: Det. Latisha Barton, L.A.P.D.:
RE: File LA.M.18711:
Lattie:
I'm e-mailing you a copy of this manuscript. We found it at the crime scene, hidden between the mattresses. Forensics confirms that it was written by Dean Anderson. We're waiting on final confirmation, but we're fairly certain that, although it had been dismembered and the head and hands were missing, the body found in the Melrose Motel belonged to him as well. We have intensified the search for Ron Wibley and his accomplice, now identified as Jennifer Anderson. Every resource the F.B.I. has available is being allocated to the manhunt.

As to the content of the attached manuscript, well, I think that it speaks volumes as to his state of mind, but I'll let you draw your own conclusions. My partner has been floating the idea that Anderson was also Wibley's accomplice and the two of them had a falling out, possibly over Jenny Anderson. Frankly, I'm inclined to agree. Let me know what you think.

Give Bill my best.
Special Agent Leroy Edwards

The Running Shadows of Netherton's Peak

Pale moonlight washed over the narrow, dirt and gravel road, turning it into a twisting silver ribbon that wound up the mountainside at a steep, thirty-degree grade. Dale Netherton concentrated on placing one foot in front of the other, fighting the nausea that lurked somewhere near the bottom of his stomach. At thirty-one he was still in fairly decent shape, but the steady climb was taking its toll. His breathing was hot and labored and his chest was on fire. Not surprising, since the closest thing he had to mountains in Florida were the speed bumps placed across the street that led to his house.

"How...much further?" he managed to gasp.

"'Bout a mile or so. Gettin' tired?" Slade Netherton, his grandfather, glanced at him with a malevolent smirk, his close-cropped white hair and beard glowing in the moonlight. Anger, a fitting companion for the nausea, raced up Dale's gullet. He took a deep breath and somehow managed to reply in a calm, even voice.

"I'm just not...used to being in the...mountains," he said, biting back the frustration. A dozen or so yards ahead, the road made a hairpin turn to the right and disappeared behind the tree line. They had been hiking for over an hour, steadily climbing the mountain that led to Slade's small cabin. Dale had argued for taking Slade's battered pickup truck, but the old man had flat out refused, insisting that driving Netherton Road in the middle of the night was an invitation to tragedy. Now, experiencing the steep grade and loose gravel firsthand, Dale could see that he was right.

David F. Gray

To his left, a few feet beyond the rough border of the road, the land disappeared, diving into a deep crevasse that ended a few hundred feet below. To his right, the mountain known locally as Netherton's Peak soared high above them. Somewhere near the top, perched on a ledge where it could survey the entire valley, was the old man's hunting cabin.

"Better get used to it," said the old man. "When I'm gone, this is yours." Dale nodded but did not speak. With both parents dead and him being an only child, he was his grandfather's only heir. Slade had invited him to visit with the purpose of going over his will. He was leaving everything...land, cabin and a respectable lump of money... to Dale. He had not specifically said, but Dale knew that he was expected to live on the land once the old man was gone. He had no intention of doing so, but had not yet told his grandfather. Slade had a fiery temper and had been known to lash out at those who crossed him. Despite being nearly seventy and a good six inches shorter than his grandson, the old man's stocky build was layered with muscle. He had a reputation for starting, and winning, countless barroom brawls.

The last thing Dale wanted to do was stoke that temper, but he had determined to tell the old man the truth before the night was over, even if it cost him his inheritance. While the money would be nice, it would mean leaving Orlando and moving to the middle of Kentucky. His career with a company that featured a certain mouse was moving forward at a pace he had never dared hope. In addition, and after a string of failed relationships, Karin had entered his life a little over two years ago. It looked like they might actually

Barriers

go the distance. He was not about to throw all of that away to perch on the top of Netherton's Peak like some kind of demented vulture.

The early September air was cool. A gust of wind hit him head on, drying the sweat on his arms and forehead. He shivered and jammed his hands into his jacket pockets. Of course, the old man noticed.

"I guess you don't have winters down there in the Sunshine State," he said. He chuckled, but his voice held a hint of mockery. He, of course, was not wearing a jacket, just a long-sleeved flannel shirt, faded jeans and worn black leather boots.

"Of course we have winters," said Dale, "but it won't get chilly until late December or early January." Slade snorted, the mockery becoming full blown derision.

"Paradise makes a man soft," he said. "Life here will toughen you up soon enough."

"Florida's not paradise," said Dale. "It's hot and humid, but it's a good place to live." He coughed hard once and took another deep breath. The burning in his chest did not abate, but at least it didn't grow worse.

"Your roots are here," said Slade, waving at the mountain rising above them. "Your family can trace its lineage back to well before the War Between the States. Why your father yanked you down to that mosquito infested hell hole I'll never understand." Again, Dale bit back a response. James Netherton had died just before Dale's twenty-third birthday. It had been sudden, and the best explanation the doctors could give him was cardiac arrest. His mother had hung on another couple of years, but the cancer she had battled in her twenties had come roaring back, taking her quickly.

"You belong here, son," said Slade. That did it. The

anger and frustration Dale had been repressing suddenly boiled over. The words came crashing out of his mouth before he could stop them.

"I'm not your son," he snapped. "And I'm barely your grandson." Slade glanced at him, smirking.

"Good," he said with a mean chuckle. "You got some Netherton grit in you after all. I was beginning to wonder if you took too much after Gloria." Hearing Slade speak his mother's name doubled Dale's anger in a heartbeat. He stopped walking and swung around to face the old man.

"My mother had more *grit* than you could imagine," he spat. "She faced her sickness with grace and peace, despite the constant pain and nausea. When the end came, she showed more courage than you'll ever have. I think if you had faced that kind of agony, you would have cried like a baby and begged God for a few minutes...a few *seconds*...free from the pain." Slade's face hardened and his fists clenched. Dale realized that he had pushed the old man too far. He took a step back, trying to brace for the inevitable attack. He could only hope that if it did come to a fight, the two of them would not go careening over the edge of the road.

"You want to be minding your manners boy," said Slade. His voice was low and threatening, but Dale was in no mood to back off.

"Why? Because you're my grandfather? In my entire life I've seen you exactly twice. Dad never talked about you. You weren't a part of his life and you aren't a part of mine." In the darkness the old man's eyes were nothing more than dark holes set deep into his skull. Dale tried to lock on to them to show the old man that he was not afraid, but his own eyes would not

Barriers

cooperate. Truth be told, he *was* afraid.

"Blood is blood, boy," said Slade. "Whether you like it or not, we're connected through that blood." Dale opened his mouth, intending to say the meanest, most hurtful thing he could think of, but something deep inside insisted that he calm down, at least until whatever business Slade needed him to complete was done. He took a deep breath and managed to steady himself.

"I'm sorry," he said, not meaning it. "I shouldn't have gone off like that, but do me a favor and leave my mother out of this." He could see that Slade wasn't buying his apology, but the old man nodded anyway.

"Never mind," he said. "I need you to see some things at the cabin. Once that's done, we can discuss my will." He turned and started walking again. "I already know that you don't intend to live here. We might as well get that out in the open."

"Fine," said Dale. He took a few quick steps to catch up to his grandfather and the two of them continued their long trek to the cabin.

"Even if it cost you everything I plan to give you?" said Slade. Dale nodded.

"I've got a good life in Orlando," he said. "I've got a woman I love and a career that brings me a lot of satisfaction. There's no way I'm giving all that up to live here."

"Making good money too, I reckon."

"Good enough," said Dale. "With more to come in the years ahead."

"There's more heritage here than just the money," said Slade. They reached the turn. A half-buried rock the size of his fist caught Dale's big toe. He stumbled

David F. Gray

but managed not to fall. They made the turn and continued up the mountain.

"I get it," said Dale, trying to mollify his grandfather. "You live in the same place long enough, it becomes a part of you." Slade shook his head.

"You *don't* get it," he said. "Your father did, but he couldn't handle it. Now that he's gone, you're all I've got." Dale threw a hateful glance at Slade.

"Did it even matter to you when he died?"

"That's a stupid question," snapped Slade.

"That's not an answer," said Dale.

"Of course it mattered," said Slade. "You have no idea how much it mattered." He glanced at his grandson. "But you will. Before this night is done, you'll understand everything. You've got my word on that."

"Fine," said Dale. "But just so we're clear, as soon as you've said what you've got to say, I'm gone. You can keep your money, your house and your land. I don't want any of it." He braced himself for another outburst, but the old man merely chuckled.

"Deal," he said. "Once you've seen what I need you to see, you can leave, if you still want to. I won't stop you." They continued their climb. Dale had left his car parked at Slade's main house, located at the base of the mountain. He intended to hike back that night, no matter how late it might be. He would drive until he found a decent motel and stay the night. In the morning he would set his course south for Orlando. Let the old man die and rot here. He was never coming back.

"There's a spot just up ahead where we can rest a bit," said Slade.

"Gettin' tired?" mocked Dale. The old man shook his

Barriers

head.

"I beat that sass out of Jimmy," he said. "I guess he didn't do you the same service. You need to learn respect, boy."

"Dad never talked about you," said Dale, "but I can see why he and Mom left. We call beating your kid abuse in my world, and what you call respect we call fear."

"A sure sign the country's goin' straight to hell," said Slade with a snort. He waved a hand at Dale. "Never mind. None of that matters now. Jimmy's gone and he's not comin' back." He waved again, this time to his right. "There," he said. "We can sit a bit. We've got time." Dale looked and saw a ragged line of five tree stumps, each about a foot high, lining the edge of the road. Slade ambled over and plopped onto the middle stump. Dale had no desire to prolong his visit, but he desperately needed a break. He followed Slade and eased himself down onto the nearest stump, deliberately maintaining space between him and his grandfather. He put his head in his hands and concentrated on his breathing. The fire in his chest cooled and the nausea subsided.

"Jimmy never told you why the Netherton family settled on this mountain, did he?" said Slade.

"He never talked about Netherton's Peak at all," said Dale.

"We took it from the Iroquois back in the early eighteen-hundreds," said Slade. "They called this land Kentahten then. Depending on who you talk to, it either means meadow, prairie, or..." his voice grew cold, "river of blood."

"You mean we stole it from them," said Dale.

David F. Gray

"Yeah, here it comes. The evil white man taking the land from the helpless natives. Well, let me tell you something boy. We didn't take anything. We won it. It was a brutal fight, and they gave as good as they got. Neither side gave an inch, and if our family hung the scalps of their braves and squaws from their belts, what of it? They did the same." Dale's nausea made a curtain call, only this time it had nothing to do with his midnight mountain climb. The idea that he was related to the brutes that spilled so much blood centuries ago, let alone being the grandson of the brute sitting next to him, was appalling.

"And that's not all we learned from them," continued Slade. Something in the way he said it got Dale's attention.

"Yeah?" he said.

"We took this land partially through brute force," said Slade. "But also by using powers we didn't understand...powers the Iroquois used, but in hindsight I don't think they really understood them either. They just had a little better control."

"Seriously?" said Dale. "You brought me up here to tell me ghost stories?"

"Nothing to do with ghosts," said Slade. Then he shrugged. "Or maybe it does. Who knows? You might think you've got a handle on life, down there in your nice clean city with your cable TV and high-speed internet, but trust me, you've got no idea how the universe works. If you did," he continued with another of his insufferable smirks, "I think you'd cry like a baby and beg God for a few more minutes...a few more *seconds*...of ignorance."

"I don't..." A hint of movement at the corner of

Barriers

Dale's eye stopped him in mid-sentence. He swiveled on the stump, looking back the way they had come. The moon was just above the tree line behind him, casting stark shadows across the road. He blinked and stared. The shadows confounded his vision, but for a moment he had been certain that someone was coming up the road behind them.

"Something wrong?" asked Slade. Dale shook his head.

"I just thought...never mind."

"You see something?"

"No...maybe," said Dale. "I...don't...what?" His eyes started watering and his vision blurred. He rubbed them and then blinked rapidly. He looked down the road again and froze. There was definitely movement. He could see a shape gliding up the road, but it was indistinct, vague. It moved between shadow and moonlight, seeming to appear and disappear, but if he concentrated...

Dale moaned. He had no choice. If he did not moan, he would have screamed. He tried to scramble to his feet and run, but his body would not cooperate. Even if he had the strength to make a mad dash up the mountain, he was locked in place. It was as if two massive hands had placed themselves on his shoulders and were pressing down. Slade reached across the space between them and grabbed his arm. His grip was iron, and his hand ice.

"It's started," he hissed. "On your soul, boy, don't move." Dale tried to pull away, but it was a futile effort. Even if he had not been frozen in place, the old man's grip was unbreakable. He could only watch as the dark form drew closer.

David F. Gray

It was human shaped...mostly. Even before it drew close Dale could tell it was tall, maybe eight or nine feet in height. Its arms swung back and forth, in sync with its long stride. There was no face, no clothing, no identifying marks of any kind. It was as if a hole had formed in his world of light and happiness, taken semi-human form, and decided to walk the land.

It drew closer. Dale suppressed another moan. He stared at the shadow, and then *into* the shadow, and saw...things. He wanted nothing more than to squeeze his eyes shut and blot out the obscene shape, but even his eyelids would not cooperate. Whatever was holding him in place had no concept of mercy and would not allow him to look away.

And still it drew closer, until it was right in front of him. Dale felt his head turn as it passed, and his eyes watched as it continued up the mountain. Just before it was engulfed in the normal shadows cast by the moonlight, it started to run. Seconds later it disappeared into the night. Tears squirted from the corners of Dale's eyes and flowed down his cheeks. He did not understand what was happening, but on a level so deep that he refused to acknowledge that it existed he knew...*knew*...that he would not be returning to Orlando, or to Karin or to his old life. He would never leave the mountain. He tried to move, and managed to lean forward a little, but the old man's grip tightened.

"This ain't over, boy," he hissed. "Stay still!" Dale managed to swivel his head and look down the road. Again he moaned. There was movement again, only now there was more than one shadow. He counted three, five, ten, and more. Each was tall and lean, but even though they appeared to be exactly like the first,

Barriers

each was different and unique in a way that filled Dale with loathing and terror.

"Please," Dale groaned. It took every ounce of strength he had left to speak that single word.

"Shut...up," growled Slade. Dale heard the barely restrained rage in his voice, but he also heard raw terror. The shadows drew closer, running in perfect unison, as if listening to a drumbeat only they could hear. The gravel crunched beneath their feet, echoing in Dale's ears *and* mind. They followed the dirt road and faded into the night. The instant they disappeared, whatever force that had been holding Dale disappeared as well. With a groan he fell forward, landing on his hands and knees. Sweat rolled down his cheeks and neck. His entire body trembled, as if it was caught in some kind of epileptic fit.

"What..." He could barely get the word out.

"It'll pass," said Slade, and for the first time Dale heard compassion in the old man's voice. "Believe me, I know. Just breathe, boy...breathe." Dale took long, deep breaths. The cool mountain air eased his trembling and slowly he regained control of his body. After a few minutes, he managed to crawl back onto the stump. Slade tried to help, but he shook him off. At that moment, he wanted to wrap his hands around the old man's throat and squeezed the life out of him. He almost lashed out to do exactly that, but his reason managed to talk him down one last time. Physically he stood no chance. The encounter with the obscene shadows had left him as weak as a newborn child. Finally, he sat up straight and glared at Slade.

"What have you done?" he demanded, his voice a harsh whisper.

"What I had to do, all those years ago," said Slade. "I took this land from the Iroquois just like I took their power"

"You? That's insane."

"I gained a lot of years, once I got a glimpse of how that power worked," continued Slade. "Centuries, in fact. But all things end. I'm at that end now, boy. The bill is coming due, and I need you to step into my place. It's part and parcel of the bargain I made." He waved at the mountain around them. "Our line is bound to this place boy, and will be until time itself ends. Think of us as guardians, or lookouts, or maybe something that can't be put into words." Somehow, Dale managed to stand. He glared down at the monster who was his grandfather.

"No," he managed to say. The old man barked a harsh laugh.

"You already know different," he said. "Once you see them, you can feel it, deep down inside. You're a part of this now. You can't leave." Dale struggled for words.

"Who...what...are they?" he finally managed to gasp. Slade shrugged.

"I may have known, but I've forgotten so much," he said. "I think I've only seen them once before, long ago." He looked up at the sky. "That would have been in the neighborhood of 1760, the year I took this mountain for my own. I had to slaughter hundreds to do it, both white and red, before I learned how to harness the power the Iroquois commanded, but harness it I did."

"That is the most batshit cr..."

"Before you finish that sentence boy," snapped

Barriers

Slade, "think about what just happened. Think real hard." Dale opened his mouth, and then closed it again. The very sight of the running shadows had damaged him beyond repair. Something sacred had been yanked out of him, and in its place was a gaping wound that he suspected would never heal.

"I thought the power of the Iroquois had something to do with the land, but I have never been more wrong," said Slade. "There's something older than the land here, boy...much older. Why it sleeps beneath this mountain, I don't know. Are there others like it, and other places like this? I don't know that either, and neither did the Iroquois, but whatever it is, it gives off a kind of power that can be harnessed. It's prolonged my life, and will prolong yours, but there's a price. You'll understa..." Slade broke off and glanced down the road. Dale followed his eyes and for the last time that night he moaned. Something else was coming up the mountain.

For an insane moment, Dale's mind told him that he was seeing a man riding a three wheeled motorcycle. He heard the engine growl and saw the wheels claw for purchase against the loose gravel of the road. The rider was too broad shouldered and too short. He was wearing a helmet, the kind without a face shield like the motorcycle gangs of the fifties wore. His face was shrouded in darkness. A long white scarf was draped around his shoulders, hanging to either side, dangerously close to the engine.

The rider looked at Dale. Then he slowly raised his right hand, fist clenched. Even in the moonlight Dale could see his middle finger slowly extend. Dale could feel his sanity slipping away. The shadow runners had been devastating, but the rider was far worse. Whatever was coming toward him was a mind killer and soul eater. It was beyond human experience and understanding. It was alien.

"What do you see, boy?" Dale had not seen Slade slide over to the stump next to him. The old man leaned against him, breathing heavily. His breath smelled of stale liquor and cigarettes. "Your mind will tell you one thing, but your eyes won't lie. What do you *see?*" Dale could not have answered if his life depended on it. He barely managed a soft whimper. The rider drew closer. "No matter," said Slade. "I'm sorry boy, but this has to be done."

The knife rammed into his back, slicing his spine and his left kidney. Slade grabbed Dale's shoulder with his free hand, grunted and shoved harder. Dale had not seen the old man carrying the knife, but judging from the way it was suddenly protruding from his stomach the blade had to be at least twelve inches long. He tried to scream in agony, but even this release was denied to him. He coughed hard and blood flew from his mouth. He tried to take a breath but his lungs would not cooperate.

"Let it come, boy," whispered Slade. "You can't stop it now. You were bound the instant you stepped foot on this mountain. Hell, you were bound the day you were born. Let it come." Dale barely heard his grandfather. His senses were failing as his body quickly shut down. He coughed up some more blood and started to fall forward, but Slade held him in his unbreakable grip. "It's almost over, boy. Let it come." Dale's consciousness faded. He opened his eyes and saw that the man on the three wheeled motorcycle had stopped in front of them. The rider's head turned toward him

Barriers

and as it did, its shape blurred and darkened. He...it...collapsed into a gaping maw that led to unthinkable and abhorrent places and times. Dale's eyes glazed over, but just before his sight failed, he looked into the utter darkness that had been the rider. In an instant both too short and too long to be measured, everything he was...his thoughts, his feelings, his memories, his very essence...was ripped from his body and dragged toward and then into that maw. He passed beyond the thin barriers of reason and reality, and began a journey that would stretch beyond time itself.

He traveled the universe, sometimes alone, sometimes with great and terrible company. He swam among the stars, witnessing the birth and death of galaxies. He beheld countless realities and possibilities. He saw wonders and terrors beyond comprehension. At length, after eternities had come and gone, he peered over the edge of all things and beheld the Great Pit. Every version of reality, every incarnation of the universe, everything that was, is and would come, teetered on the edge of the Pit. In time, it would tumble into it.

Dale Netherton stared into the Pit, and for an instant he saw the thing that lay beyond oblivion, the Devourer Of All Things. And that Devourer saw him. As tiny and insignificant...as *irrelevant*... as he was, it *saw* him. It reached through the Pit and did as its nature demanded...it devoured Dale's soul.

And finally, mercifully, it ended. A great, black curtain fell over him. His consciousness faded.

He opened his eyes. Fading red sunlight illuminated his grandfather's mountain cabin. He was lying on the dirty, bare wooden floor. Above him was a rain-stained plank roof held up by thick wooden beams darkened with age. Slowly he turned his head and saw that the cabin was mostly empty. The only furniture was a metal cot in one corner, and a small kitchen table and single chair off to his left.

For a moment, his mind was blank. Then the image of Slade's blade being thrust through his body made him cry out and the memories came crashing in. Dale Netherton, or at least the thing that used to be Dale Netherton and would in the coming centuries still think of itself as Dale Netherton, grabbed his stomach, searching for that hideous wound. His lungs sucking in air, he sat up and saw that he was naked. Looking down, he saw that there was no gaping wound, or even a scar, just unblemished skin.

Other memories...the man he had once been, the woman he had once loved, the long climb, the running shadows...flooded into his mind. Everything was still there, but it was an imperfect copy. It no longer held any meaning. His breathing slowed and he managed to stand up. The door was standing open and he moved toward it. He wobbled at first but managed to stay on his feet. He stepped through the door onto a rickety wooden porch that creaked with his weight.

The cabin stood in the middle of a small clearing. He knew without looking that the back of the cabin looked out over a wide valley. Before him, in the fading sunlight, was a small, weed infested yard that ended in a nearly impenetrable tree line. The only opening was the end of the dirt road that led down the mountain to a life that was no longer his. Heedless of his nakedness, he sat down at the edge of the porch and put his feet on the cool ground. Far below, something slept.

Barriers

He waited.

Darkness fell and still he waited.

The night sky spun overhead and still he waited.

Finally, he saw them. The running shadows had returned, only now they were no longer running. They walked slowly, even solemnly, into the yard. Seeing them no longer filled Dale with terror and loathing. He understood, at least on some level, that the shadows were nothing more than an unconscious manifestation of the Sleeper beneath Netherton's Peak.

They moved toward the cabin, breaking into two lines. They took their stations, forming a corridor between the end of the road and the cabin like some kind of profane honor guard. Dale watched in silence, already knowing what was to come.

At the last came the Rider. Now Dale saw It for what It truly was, and even then he felt no terror. For the moment at least, he was beyond such things. Next to the Rider cowered Slade Netherton. His head was down and his shoulders slumped. Like Dale, the old man was naked, but his once powerful body was now withered and emaciated. Like Dale, he was returning from an impossibly long journey. And like Dale, his story was not yet over. It had, in fact, barely begun.

The Rider, that hole in time and space that was nevertheless sentient, beckoned. Obediently, Dale rose. He moved forward, walking between the shadow runners with utter calm. As he drew close, Slade looked up and saw him.

"Dale...don't. Please don't." Dale continued to walk toward him and the old man began to sob. "I didn't know. I couldn't remember. Please don't do this. You still have a choice." He was wrong, of course. Dale's will was no longer his own. Slade's blade had seen to that. The Devourer beyond the Great Pit had seen to it as well, when it had consumed everything that made Dale the man he used to be.

He reached out. The Rider placed Slade's blade into his hand. Slade moaned, much in the same way Dale had moaned when he had seen the first shadow. Dale did not hesitate. He stepped forward and rammed the blade through Slade's throat, the force so great that it burst out the back of his neck. Slade's blood spurted from both sides. His breathing stopped and his eyes turned milky white. It's work now done, Dale returned the blade to the rider. He looked at the old man.

"They took your memory, just as they'll take mine," he said in a voice that was devoid of any emotion. "You thought that you were making a trade...me for you...but you were just completing an unbreakable cycle that I will be forced to continue." He glanced at the Rider. "They'll take my memories too, and in a few centuries I'll complete this same cycle, with my future son or grandson." Now as dead as Dale had been, Slade stirred. He looked up at Dale with his white, empty eyes. "Goodbye, Grandfather," said Dale. "Whatever is waiting for you, I hope it hurts."

Slade's dead face contorted with a look of ultimate terror. Then the emptiness that was the Rider slowly engulfed him. Dale knew that the old man would be dragged deep beneath Netherton's Peak, where he would be slowly devoured by the Sleeper. In time, Dale's turn would come, as would his progeny. The Sleeper would feast on the emptiness the Devourer had left within him, and through it all he would be aware.

In time, perhaps in thousands of years, the Sleeper

Barriers

would be filled. It would rise from beneath its mountain haven and dive into the stars. It would join countless of its kind in a mad dash to the End and hurl itself into the Great Pit. That was its nature, and it could no more choose to do otherwise than Dale could now choose to leave Netherton's Peak.

The Rider and Slade disappeared. Immediately the shadows started moving. They walked past Dale, heading toward the road. By the time they reached it, they were running. They disappeared into the night, waiting for the fullness of time when they would return to repeat the cycle. Dale watched them go and then turned and walked back to the cabin. He was guardian of Netherton's Peak now, and would remain so until it was his time to descend and feed the Sleeper.

In the bedroom, he found clothes that fit him perfectly. He dressed and went outside. By the time he sat down on the porch again, his memories of his grandfather's fate, along with those of his cosmic journey, had faded. He stared at the night sky, ablaze with countless stars, unaware that he had traveled among those very stars. He took a long, deep breath. The breath became a yawn and he realized that he was exhausted. He went inside to sleep.

David F. Gray

The Stars Denied

Final Transmission
Col. Jillian T. Davis
Cmdr, U.E.S.S. Concepcion
Pluto Expeditionary Force
June 21st, 2287

I am setting communications on wide band, with no encryption, and I'm going to talk as long as I am able. Maybe the fools who sent us here will be able to block this message. Maybe it will get through. Even if it does, it will likely be dismissed as the ravings of a madwoman, or more likely a madman.

I am standing at the crest of a low, sloping hill. Looking to the horizon, I see a dime sized glowing orb. Its dull light illuminates the swirling methane and gives Pluto's toxic atmosphere a beautiful purplish-blue tint. Hanging above and to my left, its mottled gray surface dominating the black sky, is Charon, Pluto's largest moon.

It's a breathtaking vista, but I did not climb this hill to marvel at the local sights. I came here to take one last look at my home. I lower another filter over my visor, hoping to cut out most of the glare of that far away sun. Finally I see it; a tiny speck of light peeking through the swirling clouds. I stare at it, my heart breaking with the certainty that I will never set foot on it again. All our hopes, our dreams, our history, everything we have become, it all resides on that tiny, insignificant speck.

If I could somehow wave my arms and make that glowing pinpoint grow, I would see stunning blue

Barriers

oceans, green and brown continents, and swirling, mesmerizing weather patterns. Crossing the terminator, the soft darkness of night will come alive with the blazing lights of countless cities. For just a moment, I close my eyes and imagine I can hear the murmur of Earth's five billion souls as they go about their everyday routines, living in relative peace. I try to transport myself across the billions of miles to join them, but when I open my eyes, I am still standing on this lonely hill on a desolate world at the very edge of our solar system.

Here is a terrible truth.

Humanity will never reach the stars.

If I ever said that in public I would be crucified. After all, we are the dauntless human race. We are the people who managed to survive the Great Calamity of 2202, when nearly two thirds of our population was eradicated. We are the people who scraped and clawed our way out of decades of darkness to build a new and better civilization. We are the people who discovered zero-point energy, which not only gave us enough free power to light every city on earth for a thousand years but also nullified the greatest obstacle to space travel...gravity. We are the people who colonized the moon, Mars and the asteroid belt.

We are a race in constant motion, always moving outward, our sights set on interstellar space. The slogan of fifty years ago still resonates today. 'Today the nine, tomorrow the stars.' That's not accurate, of course. Pluto remains downgraded to a planetoid, but 'The Nine' has been stuck in our collective consciousness for centuries. Besides, with over four billion miles between it and Earth, there has never been a relevant reason to

David F. Gray

come here.

Until now.

There were eleven of us on the Concepcion, a sturdy Magellan class exploration ship. We could have easily accommodated a crew of fifty or more, but the general consensus was that our mission needed to be accomplished in absolute secrecy, so the fewer involved the better.

There were also practical reasons for a small crew. Pluto was not just a jaunt around the block, like Mars. Even with a sturdy ship and a virtually unlimited power supply, it was a highly dangerous mission. Power might be unlimited, but consumables were not. The Concepcion was jammed to the rafters with supplies, and even then we were on a tight timetable. Add to that the fact that, the greater the distance, the greater the potential, or rather the probability, for disaster. Our mission would last nearly five years, and that danger increased with every passing day.

I should mention my crew. Unless this message gets past Earth's security nets, the knowledge of this mission will be scuttled as thoroughly as the Concepcion. I am sure that explanations for our deaths were planned before we ever left orbit. They deserve better. They were good people; smart, tough and professional. And they were my family, so I have to try.

Jim Halloway was my exec. He had a wife and two children on Mars. Shakia Duvall was our chief engineer. She was a third-generation belter, as tough as they come. Greg Sampson, Earth-born, was our navigator and all-around funny man. He was a key reason that we stayed sane during the trip out. Jacob Hill was our assistant engineer and Shakia's lover. We

Barriers

never caught them at it, but I'm fairly certain that engineering was covered with their combined DNA. Sandra Simpson, mission specialist (biology), was a veteran of fifteen deep space missions. She never said much, which we all found refreshing. In a ship of talkative alpha personalities, silence is a thing of beauty. Craig and Kelly Fauset were also mission specialists (archeology). Unlike the rest of us, they were well into their fifties. Their qualifications spoke for themselves. They became our unofficial godparents.

The last three were military; Colonel Sam Baker, Captain Daniel Frost and Lieutenant Lakshay Divit. Lakshay doubled as our doctor. I was in command of the ship and the flight to and from Pluto. Sam was in command of the mission once we hit dirt. The three of them integrated well with the rest of the crew.

None of us had volunteered, but we all knew where we were going and why. There was no 'need to know' crap that sometimes plagues highly classified operations. I should also mention that Sam and I were lovers. We were not *in* love. Rather, we were good friends who did not want to spend the long years alone in our beds. Add to that the fact that we were equal in rank and it made perfect sense to the both of us.

We weren't saints, of course. We got on each other's nerves and there was more than one shouting match, but things never got out of hand. We understood that the only chance we had of getting home was to work together and trust each other. We also understood the stakes.

You see, there's something on Pluto, and it's not *of* Pluto. It's not life. Nothing so obscene could ever be labeled life, but it is aware, and it is intelligent.

David F. Gray

History tells of the New Horizons probe and its stunning pictures of Pluto. We saw towering mountains covered with ice along with vast plains. We marveled at this tiny, frozen, dark world, so far away, but we would not visit it again for over two hundred and sixty-five years.

Ambassador Four was tasked to do a quick flyby as it made its way out of the solar system, carrying yet another message of greeting and friendship from the good people of Earth. We had a couple of centuries to improve resolution, transmission strength and data transference. It paid off big time. Tucked deep into the base of one of Pluto's massive mountain ranges was a city.

At least, that's what the experts called it. Its initial designation was PA-1...Pluto Anomaly One...and every one of us desperately hoped that there was not a PA-2. Some genius suggested is unofficial name be Persephone, after Pluto's lover, but no one bought in to that for a second. To name anything so...wrong...after someone who brought light to the underworld was obscene. They called it Nix, for the goddess of darkness and night. True, that is also the name of one of Pluto's moons, but the name fit.

When I was read into the mission and shown the pictures, I nearly lost my dinner. Even with Ambassador Four's amazing resolution, the flyby had been fast and the images, especially when magnified, were somewhat grainy. I was grateful for that. If they had been any sharper, I think I may have run screaming from the briefing room like a terrified child who had just discovered that the monster under her bed was real. I am attaching as many of our files as I can jam into

Barriers

this data stream, so everyone can see for themselves.

There was an organic feel to Nix, as if it had been grown instead of built. Just glancing at the pictures made me think of a tumor sinking its roots deep into the pristine Plutonian surface. Best estimates judged that it was maybe fifty kilometers long and half as wide, but there was no symmetry or order. The 'buildings' seemed to have no corners and flat walls, but at the same time there were sharp edges and flat surfaces. According to the data, the spires near the center of the city were at least three kilometers high, but they did not go straight up. They had been built at such ridiculous angles that, even in Pluto's low gravity, it should have been impossible for them to exist. I held the pictures in my trembling hands and fancied that I could feel the entire city...that *thing*...throb with dark, malignant power. My God, it was so alien.

There have been a lot of stories told throughout the centuries about the arrival of extraterrestrial beings to our little blue and green world; novels, movies, holos. Sometimes they're friendly. Sometimes they come to pick a fight, but no matter how they are portrayed, we at least can understand their motives because these stories are written by humans.

That damned city told another story. Whatever built it was beyond our understanding. Not so much advanced, perhaps, but so very alien. I am not ashamed to say that I argued against this mission, and I was not alone. Those who agreed with me saw terror and obscenity. Those who disagreed could only think of one word...interstellar...because it was beyond obvious that whatever built that city was not from our tiny corner of the galaxy.

David F. Gray

The interstellar crowd won. I flatly refused the mission, and I'm fairly certain that any of my peers would have done the same if they had been given the chance. Instead, I went to sleep in my apartment and woke up on the Concepcion, already six months into the mission. It was the same for my crew, including our military contingent. We had all been conscripted, placed in induced comas, and shipped out like so much cargo. A minimal medical staff had kept watch over us, and a minimal flight crew put us on course for Pluto. They were taken off less than twelve hours before we were awakened.

I knew the instant I regained consciousness what had happened. We all did. I immediately got Jim and Shakia working out a return course, but less than an hour after our awakening, we got our orders. We were to land on Pluto, as near to Nix as possible, and carry out a survey mission. Our supplies would allow us to stay a maximum of thirty-two days and we were expected to use every second of that window. If we aborted the mission, the Concepcion would be destroyed. If we cut our stay short, the Concepcion would be destroyed. If we...well, you get the idea. We fought it every step of the way, but in the end, we were going to Pluto.

My time is nearly gone. I have to make this fast.

Needless to say, we made it. The trip out, and even our landing on Pluto, was uneventful. The crew spent a great deal of time combing through line after line of code, searching for the destruct command our superiors had placed into our system. We never found it. We made landfall, flying solely on instruments, secured the ship and very reluctantly turned our attention to Nix.

Barriers

We landed less than two hundred yards away, so it was not only detectable by our sensor net but easily visible through every view port on the starboard side of the ship. We had kept them closed on the way down, not out of safety concerns but out of a real fear for our sanity. An hour after we landed, we gathered in the wardroom and braced ourselves. Even through the bulkhead, we could all feel something vile radiating from Nix. We knew that what we were going to see was going to damage us in some way, but we had each other and we hoped that that would be enough. I nodded to Jim and he hit the exterior lights and raised the viewport shields.

The next thing I remember is pounding the control panel, screaming for the ports to shut. I have always considered myself a tough, well-trained professional, able to handle even the most dire situations without losing my calm. By the time the ports slammed shut I was weeping uncontrollably. A few of the others had fallen to the deck, covering their eyes. Craig and Kelly bolted for their quarters. Sam was on his knees, staring at the deck. Both Daniel and Lakshay were unconscious.

I am not going to describe what we saw. The files I am sending speak for themselves, and I can only hope that they are enough to convince the idiots who sent us here to *never* send another ship to Pluto.

We slowly came back to ourselves. We didn't recover. We would never recover. Even if we were allowed to go home, we would forever carry the open wounds Nix had carved into our minds and worse, our souls. Yeah, I said souls. You see, that's one of the little discoveries I've made on Pluto. We have a soul.

David F. Gray

We were all of the same mind. Let them destroy the Concepcion, but we were not getting a centimeter closer to Nix. We would gather as much data as we could through passive scans, but we were not going to transmit it. If they wanted it, they would have to let us come home. If not, they could blow us to hell, and we would be grateful. We did our best to concentrate on our respective tasks. I manned the bridge, composing a message to Earth. We would record the message together, to show our solidarity. No matter what, we were raising ship in twelve hours.

We finished our tasks and met in the wardroom. My crew was behind me, and Sam stood at my side. We all agreed that Sam and I would speak for everyone. We recorded our ultimatum and set it to transmit an hour after liftoff. It would take about six hours for our signal to get to Earth. Even if whoever was listening was authorized to immediately destroy us, that gave us a solid twelve hours to get the hell away from Pluto. When we were finished, we got back to work prepping the ship.

Not long after, I felt it. I was alone on the bridge, triple checking our launch trajectory. At first, it was a faint itch, like a spider brushing its forelegs against the back of my neck. I scratched it, but it did not go away. For an instant, I chalked it up to stress, but just after I lowered my hand, that gentle tickling quickly transformed into a dull, throbbing pressure. Like I said, I'm well trained. Acting on that training, I reached out to the intercom to call for help, but my body froze. The entire episode had lasted mere seconds, but it was already too late.

The pressure increased, until I felt a barrier give

Barriers

way. It was an ancient barrier, I think. Most of us are not even aware of it, even though it has surrounded us and protected us since we have walked upright on our planet. It's a barrier that guards our very essence, that thing that makes each of us unique and irreplaceable. It's powerful, but mine crumbled instantly. I was invaded...*defiled*. A presence older than our sun and alien beyond imagination poured into my body, and in a space of time too small to be measured, it explored me, and it *knew* me.

Vile energy surrounded me, cocooning my body, mind and soul in an unbreakable shell. My consciousness was seized, bound and shoved into a dark, bottomless well. I could peek out of my eyes and hear with my ears, but my body was no longer my own. That body stood and made its way through the ship into the aft airlock. I was made to get into an environment suit, and as soon as my helmet was secure, the thing inside me started the depressurization cycle. Seconds later I heard Sam's voice coming through my helmet, ordering me to stand down.

As soon as the cycle was complete, the outer door opened and the ramp extended. Without any hesitation, my body walked down that ramp and I became the first human to step foot on Pluto's surface. There, just two hundred yards away, Nix waited. The thing controlling me kept my eyes fixed on it, and even jammed into that dark well in my mind, I could not turn away. I screamed. I pounded non-existent fists against my equally non-existent prison, begging to be released, but I...*we*... kept walking.

My screams grew weaker as I felt myself changing. Remember what I said about having a soul? We really do possess one, and contrary to current belief, it really is immortal. I have come to understand that it can't be destroyed, but like any other type of matter or energy, it can change form.

Seconds after this change began, my hands moved to the seals on my helmet. Again I screamed, to no avail. My hands moved quickly, surely, and moments later they grabbed both sides of my helmet and pulled it off of my head.

I don't know how long it took me to die. Probably a matter of seconds, but when you are in agony, a single moment lasts an eternity. My blood roared in my ears as I was simultaneously boiled by the hard radiation and frozen by the minus two hundred forty degrees Celsius temperature. As I burned, my soul was ripped out of my body and dragged toward Nix. Despite the fact that I no longer possessed a physical form, I could see my body, minus helmet, still standing. I will not describe my face.

My perception was enhanced a hundred-fold. When I had seen those first photos of Nix, I had thought of it as a malignant tumor. My perception had been spot on. Nix was a living thing; a single entity burrowing like a tick into Pluto's surface. Ambassador Four had only captured a fraction of its actual size. With my enhanced sight, I could see how Nix had completely possessed Pluto. Its roots ran like great trunks throughout the entire planet, all leading to a central, throbbing mass buried deep in its core. In every possible way, Nix *was* Pluto.

All this and more I saw as I was dragged beneath the surface. I felt madness closing in and welcomed it, but Nix had other plans. Another barrier formed around me,

Barriers

only this barrier kept the madness at bay. Nix wanted its new toy sane.

Downward I plunged, until I reached the central mass. Without hesitation, I was dragged into that mass. My sight failed and I floated in utter darkness. Then quickly, ruthlessly, I was dissected. My mind, my thoughts, my feelings, were sliced apart, held up for inspection, rearranged and then jammed back together. Through it all, I begged and pleaded for mercy, but these concepts were as alien to Nix as Nix was to me.

I had foolishly believed that dying unprotected on Pluto was the worst that could happen to me, but having my soul mutilated was beyond agony, and even that was not the end. Nix prodded and explored every bit of me, down to the tiniest speck of my consciousness, but in doing so, revealed an infinitesimal part of itself to me. I understood.

God help me, I understood.

I don't know how long I was tormented. Time ceased to have any meaning. Subjectively it could have been a day or a thousand years, but eventually I was reassembled and sent back to the Concepcion. I rose to the surface, and when I saw my ship, I wept. It was bound by the same power that possessed me. I knew the instant I was possessed that I was lost, but I had hoped my crew might still manage to escape. Now I understood that none of us would be going home. We were doomed the instant we landed on Pluto.

I passed through the Concepcion's hull and entered the bridge. It seemed that only hours had passed since my death. Sam was there, along with Jim. They were in shock, but they were somehow pushing through it and working feverishly, prepping the ship for liftoff. Nix was not subtle. The obscene power that had enslaved me ruthlessly snatched both Jim and Sam. I could only watch as their souls were imprisoned and then ripped from their bodies. Maybe it was the physical connection we shared, but as he was carried way, Sam sensed me.

Jill? I wanted to scream at the shock and terror contained in that single thought, but Nix was not finished. I was jammed into Sam's body, and suddenly I once again possessed physical senses. Moving with a will not my own, I stepped over to the engineering console. Nix had learned everything it needed to know, and within minutes, I...it...had overridden the controls and set the ship for self-destruct.

The alarms began to blare. Seconds later Shakia and Greg bolted onto the bridge. They didn't even have time to assess the situation. Nix dragged them out of their bodies and into itself. I felt it grab the rest of the crew, and could only watch as their bodies quickly died. I understood that the soul can survive without the body, but the body cannot long survive without the soul.

After that, I was left alone. I had been used as a blueprint and a conduit for Nix to take the rest of the crew. Now that it had them, it ignored me. I had a little time, but only a little. I knew that my reprieve was temporary. I was forever bound to Nix. I managed to don Sam's environment suit, grab a portable communicator, get to the surface, and climb this hill before the ship exploded. So here I am, alone, trapped in a body not my own and staring up at a far-off world that is no longer my home. My only hope is that this transmission will get through, and that it will prevent any further expeditions to Pluto. If that happens, then

Barriers

the human race might have a little time left. Maybe it doesn't really matter. As a race, we are done.

Here's what I learned from Nix.

Remember the barrier that surrounded my soul, the one Nix obliterated when it took me? There is second barrier, only this one encases our entire solar system. Despite the difference in size, they are much alike, but my 'soul barrier' is...was... a natural part of me. The big one is artificial, and very old. Even Nix does not remember when it was created. I do know that Earth was nothing more than a violent primordial rock that would not bring forth life for at least another billion years. This barrier was erected to allow that life to form and flourish.

In essence, our world is nothing more than a massive game preserve, waiting to be harvested by beings older than the stars. When the time comes, Nix will destroy the barrier and these beings will sweep through our system, cover our world and devour our souls. But those souls will not be destroyed. They will join with those like Nix. They will take us apart, explore us and feed on us for eternity.

And not just those who are unfortunate enough to be living at the time. You see, the barrier has a second purpose. It acts as a container, keeping the soul of every human who has ever lived within its boundaries. From that far off time when the first human somehow formed the first soul, it has been catching them at death and storing them, waiting for the harvest. These souls do not sleep. They are awake, and they are aware. They know what is in store for them.

That harvest is coming. Maybe we have a few centuries left, but I know for sure that it will happen within the next thousand years. Even death cannot save us. Even if we somehow managed to develop interstellar technology, there is a third purpose to the barrier. It will not allow organic matter to pass. We can send all the probes we want, but we will never leave our solar system. At the appointed time, the barrier will collapse, and humanity will meet its collective fate.

And I will be there to see it. When Nix destroys the barrier, I will be there. When these beings descend upon earth, I will be there. When every human soul that has ever existed is harvested, I will be there. When they move on to the next world, and the next, and the next, I will be there. I will see stars born and die. I will see this universe collapse and burn, only to be born anew. Of course, by then any shred of my memory will be long gone. Jill Davis will be nothing more than a single cell floating in the great mind of some ancient being that will never die.

Stay away from Pluto. Whoever lands here will simply be taken as I was taken...as my crew was taken. Live what life you have left. Treasure each and every year, day, minute and second. Savor the time, because what comes after is torment beyond imagination.

My time is done. Nix knows what I am doing, but it doesn't care. In a few seconds it will drag me back into the bowels of Pluto. Maybe I will be able to sense my crew, at least a little. It might make the hell that awaits more bearable, but I doubt it will happen. As I said, Nix knows nothing of mercy or compassion. Please, listen to me. Leave Pluto alone. For the love of humanity, leave Pluto a....

* * *

Barriers

Summary of the final report of Colonel Sam Baker, prepared for Admiral Sarah Chambers.

Admiral:

Here is the transcript of Colonel Baker's final transmission. I can say without hesitation that our team of analysts, including two of the best psychiatric profilers on the planet, are at a loss to explain his actions. There is nothing in any of his evaluations that would remotely suggest this kind of behavior. We can only surmise that he somehow assumed the persona of Colonel Jillian Davis out of some deep sense of guilt. The data burst from Baker included telemetry from the Concepcion. It shows that it was Baker himself who initiated the self-destruct. Whether this was due to some kind of influence from Nix or the result of Baker losing his grip on reality we cannot say. The good news is that we were able to intercept his transmission. It will not be made public.

The only way we will ever get any real answers is to send another expedition to Pluto. Our recommendation is that it consist of at least three ships, each with a full flight crew and military contingent. They will be tasked with the joint objectives of combing through the wreckage of the Concepcion and the exploration of Nix. Concepcion's data storage units should be intact. We were careful to protect them in case the ship was destroyed.

As for Nix, we have no answers. We believe that the secrets to interstellar travel could very well be hidden within it. Despite Colonel Baker's ravings, we strongly recommend a thorough and prolonged exploration of the city.

David F. Gray

The Estate

You don't find the dead.
The dead find you.

I stumbled into that damned bar after one really bad day and four too many drinks. The bad day was courtesy of that vile, self-absorbed creature commonly known as a celebrity. Come to think of it, so were the drinks.

I was covering a major network's fall media show out in Los Angeles. After a lot of bowing and scraping, I had managed to land a short interview with the star of a fairly popular television drama. I was in place fifteen minutes early, and of course the star was almost half an hour late. He did not want to be there, that much was certain. The actors who attend these events do so because they are contractually obligated to promote their work, but at least most of them make an effort to be cordial. This guy couldn't have cared less. I asked my questions and got short, surly answers. As soon as the interview was over, I asked if I could get a picture with him.

"There's a thousand of you local yokels here, and one of me," he replied, not bothering to hide his scorn. "Find someone else to hang on your office wall back in Hick Land." With that he got up and stalked off, his agent and publicist in tow.

I had known coming in that I was going to have to put up with a few arrogant SOBs. It goes with being an entertainment reporter for a local television station like WFAC (serving the greater Tampa Bay Area). Still, his words hurt. There are four movie scripts gathering

Barriers

digital dust on my computer back home, with another in the works. I have been trying to break into the 'big time' for twenty years, with nothing to show for it but a lot of heartbreak. At forty-five, I still have time, but each passing year brings less and less hope. WFAC could very well be the best that I will ever do for myself and my family.

Back at my hotel (The Quality Inn Suites, *not* the Hyatt or Hilton; my boss will only go so far) I dumped my things into my room and made straight for the bar. I had nowhere to go until my flight home the next night, and was determined to get blind, stinking drunk. I don't drink a lot, as a rule, but as I said, the actor's words had struck a nerve. I suddenly saw myself at WFAC for the rest of my life, and the prospect was beyond depressing.

The hotel bar was on the far side of the small lobby. It was called The Clipper Ship, and so naturally was decked out in a seafaring motif. The tables and chairs were all made out of plastic molded to look like driftwood, and there was a huge, brightly lit saltwater fish tank sitting against one wall, filled with multi-colored tropical fish. The bar ran along the wall opposite the entrance.

The only thing that I cared about was the darkness. There was barely enough light to navigate past the tables. It was just past six, and the place was almost deserted. I found a table in a dark corner, ordered a double vodka and got started on my first drunk in ten years.

By the time I finished my second drink (scotch, straight up; I like variety), I was getting that pleasant buzz that meant that if I tried hard enough, I could probably find my way back to my room. On this night, that was nowhere near good enough.

Drink three was a martini. I started in on drink number four...gin and tonic, no ice...and settled back into my chair, enjoying the ride. I let my eyes drift over the small lounge, not really noticing anything. I glanced at the fish tank, and then blinked. Just off to the left was an entrance to another lounge. I had not paid much attention to my surroundings when I came in. The Clipper Ship was just another hotel bar, unremarkable in every aspect.

This second lounge looked different. From what I could see through the open double doors, it had an elegant feel that was totally out of character with the rest of the hotel. Shiny dark marble flooring reflected the soft light provided by expensive looking chandeliers. I could see another bar far in the back...this place was fairly large...that seemed to be made of solid oak. It had an honest to goodness brass foot rail and a dozen or so comfortable looking leather-bound stools. Behind the bar, lined up like obedient soldiers waiting to be called into action, were hundreds of bottles on four long shelves. A sign above the doors, made with even more brass, proclaimed in a bold font that I was looking at THE ESTATE.

The evening crowd was filtering into the Clipper Ship, but The Estate appeared to be deserted. I glanced at my watch and was surprised to see that it was past eight. Granted, I had been nursing my drinks, but it did not feel as if two hours had passed. Curious, I lurched to my feet, took a moment to make sure that the room was only spinning in one direction, and made my way over to the entrance. A receptionist's podium stood off

Barriers

to the left, but it was deserted. Moving past it, I peeked inside, but could see no one sitting at the few dozen round ornate wooden tables that filled the room.

My first impression had been correct. The Estate was a great deal more elegant than the Clipper Ship. It appeared to be closed, however, and with a pang of regret, I turned to go. The receptionist, suddenly appearing at the podium, nodded and smiled at me.

"Would you like a table, sir," she asked nicely, "or would you rather sit at the bar?" Startled, I took a step backward. She was young and pretty, dark haired and pale skinned, almost certainly a celebrity in training. Who isn't in this town?

"I – I – I…" Taking a deep breath, I tried to compose myself. I was drunk, but not *that* drunk. She had not been there thirty seconds ago. She must have been in the Clipper Ship, perhaps getting change or something, and returned when she saw me enter. My head cleared slightly and I tried again.

"I thought you were closed," I said, my voice just a little slurred.

"Oh no, sir," she replied gravely. "We're open. We're always open. Table for one?"

"Thanks," I said, "but if it's all the same, I'll just have a quick drink at the bar." She nodded and waved me on. I turned back to the bar, but for just a moment, wavered. Something inside me wanted to go back to my dark corner, order another drink and finish what I had started. I glanced over my shoulder and blinked. The hostess had disappeared again.

She's a nimble little minx. I heard Bill Murray's voice in my head and giggled. No doubt she had ducked back into the Clipper Ship to finish her errand. I looked back through the doors, but for some odd reason, the hotel lounge seemed even darker than before. I could barely make out the fish tank off to the left. Everything else seemed to be shrouded in shadows. The idea of going back into that soulless, plastic infested den was suddenly repulsive, and with new resolve I turned my back on it and headed to the bar.

The bartender, a sturdy, older man with dark hair graying at the temples, waved at me. I studded over the fact that, like the hostess, I had not noticed him before, but shrugged it off and ambled over.

"Sir?" he asked professionally. He was wearing black pants, white shirt with the sleeves rolled up, and a black vest. I noted his green, oval shaped name tag, identifying him as Sid.

"Double vodka, no ice," I said, sliding onto one of the stools and leaning against the polished wood.

"Yes sir." Sid was good. In just a few seconds, I had my drink. I turned around and eyed the empty tables.

"Slow night," I said. I really didn't want to start a conversation, but it seemed rude not to at least make an attempt at small talk.

"For now," said Sid. "The usual crowd will filter in soon." I swiveled back to face him.

"I would have thought that a place like this wouldn't have a usual crowd," I said. He lifted an eyebrow. "I mean, don't you have mostly event traffic, with the convention center this close?"

"Mostly," said Sid with a shrug. "But we have our regulars, like any other bar."

"And they'll be coming in soon?"

"In a way," replied Sid. "They're always here, poor souls." He shrugged again. "I have no idea why they

Barriers

stay here, but that's their business. I just serve the drinks."

"I must be more drunk than I thought," I said. "I didn't understand a word of what you just said."

"It doesn't matter," said Sid. "The Estate found you. For that, I'm truly sorry." He glanced over my shoulder and nodded. I turned toward the door but there was no one there, not even the receptionist.

"What the hell does that mean?" When he did not answer, I turned back to the bar. He was nowhere in sight. *Huh?* I looked around, but there was no trace of him. Taking a good-sized swig of my drink, I told myself that I really was too drunk to be out in public, but I was suddenly uncomfortable. Although The Estate was empty, I had the absurd impression that I was now being watched. All of a sudden, my dark little corner of the Clipper Ship did not seem that bad. I decided to go back.

"Could you talk to me? Please?" The feminine voice came from my left. I glanced at the nearest table and saw a young woman, probably no older than twenty-five, sitting alone. She had not been there just moments ago.

"I'm…I'm sorry?" She was pretty; long blonde hair, petite figure, with lovely features, but I've been married for over twenty years. I've never cheated on Carol, and I had no intention of starting now.

"Please," she begged, her voice cracking. I slid off my stool and took a step toward her. The look on her face spoke of such loneliness that I instinctively wanted to help.

"What's wrong?" I asked.

"Just talk to me." Tears started down her cheeks.

She turned away, as if ashamed.

"Look," I said, reaching into my pocket for my mobile, "maybe I can call someone. They can come and get you. Do you know anyone…" She turned back to face me and I screamed. I stumbled backward, slamming into the table behind me. Gone was the beautiful young girl. The hair, clothes and figure were all the same, but the face…

"TALK TO ME!" The face was a void, a blank. No eyes, no nose, no other features, nothing but a yawning chasm of a mouth. "TALK TO ME!" I screamed again and stumbled away. Somewhere inside my mind, I was still trying to tell myself that I was drunk and hallucinating, but I wasn't buying it. I had wandered into a place that was not meant for the living. Death was in this room. Death *was* this room.

And it was hungry.

I staggered toward the entrance. I could still see the Clipper Ship through the open doors, but now it seemed...*thin.* Only the glimmer of the fish tank assured me that it was actually there. I passed another table, and a hand shot out of nowhere, and I mean nowhere, and grabbed my wrist. I spun around and found myself facing a man about my age. He was short and disturbingly obese, like the Monty Python puking scene obese.

"Tell my wife," he screamed at me, his face just inches from my own. His breath stank of stale vomit and I felt my gorge rise. "Tell my wife! Tell my wife! Tell my wife!" I tried to pull away, but he was too strong. He yanked me into the chair next to him. I fell forward, and my head hit the table. For just an instant, darkness closed in. I blinked and my eyes cleared. The

Barriers

fat man had disappeared, but now the room was full of people, and they were all screaming at me. An old woman with rotting skin begged me to take her away to heaven. A boy, no more than five, cried for his mother. Three girls, perhaps seventeen, kept shouting 'I'm sorry, I'm sorry' over and over again in perfect unison.

They were constantly fading in and out, each one only visible for a moment, but for every one that left, two more took their place. The noise was overwhelming, and not just because it was loud. There are things we are not meant to see or hear, at least while we are alive. Their presence assaulted my innermost being. I could feel their spirits reaching out for my own... reaching out and *reaching in*. My soul was being invaded, tormented and brutalized.

I slapped my hands against my ears, but it did not help. A thousand damned souls were demanding my attention, breaching the barrier between life and death. I lurched out of the chair and stumbled toward the entrance. It seemed impossibly far away now, and I instinctively knew that I had seconds to escape. The noise increased, and figures crowded all around me. Hands reached out and tried to grab my arms, shoulders and legs, but somehow I kept going. By the time I got to the entrance, all I could see of the Clipper Ship was the fish tank.

The receptionist was back at her stand, only now her eyes were empty. I don't mean devoid of life. I mean empty. They were black holes, eyeless sockets, and for just an instant, I looked into those sockets.

I saw Hell.

Then she smiled and spoke to me. I screamed again and threw myself through an opening that was barely

David F. Gray

there.

I fell hard onto the worn carpet of the Clipper Ship. Stunned, I could only lay there, gasping for breath. After a few moments, a pair of strong hands grabbed me by the shoulders and pulled me up. I was certain that the dead of The Estate had come for me, but it was only one of the waiters from the Clipper Ship.

"It's all right, sir," he said with practiced ease. "You signed for your drinks, so you're square here. Let's call someone and get you to your room." I looked over his shoulder, knowing what I would see. The fish tank was still there, but of course there was no sign of The Estate. With an effort, I pushed away from the waiter.

"I can find my way," I muttered. He eyed me professionally. What he saw must have assured him that I was at least sober enough to get to my room. He nodded and went back to work.

I didn't waste any time. I changed my airline reservations to the red eye for that night. I made a quick call to Carol to tell her I'd be in around three a.m. I would take a cab home.

That was six months ago.

I made it home and tried to settle back into my life, but of course, that has been impossible. I've been touched by the dead, literally. Once that happens, nothing is ever the same. I wake up in the middle of the night, every night, fighting to get out of some nightmare that I can never remember. As I claw my way back into consciousness, I glimpse, for just an instant, the entrance to The Estate. Sometimes it's by my dresser, sometimes it's replaced the door to my closet, but it's always there, waiting for me to return.

Remember when I said that the hostess spoke to me

Barriers

just before I escaped? I looked into those empty chasms that had once been eyes, and all that I could see was loneliness; utter, complete loneliness. Surely there cannot be a better definition of hell.

You can never really leave, she said, and her voice was the voice of the damned.

Right now, it's two in the morning and I'm sitting in front of the computer in my study. I woke up about an hour ago. I saw the entrance to The Estate again, only this time it took a long time to fade. I lay in bed, next to Carol, staring at the double doors with the expensive brass letters. My time is growing short.

Last week, I went in for my annual check-up. Yesterday I got a call from my doctor, asking me to drop by for a few additional tests. *It's just a spot on the x-ray, on your left lung. Probably nothing, but we need to be sure.*

I've tried my best to live a good life. I've been a faithful husband and loving father. I've given to charities and tried to make my small corner of the world a little better for having been in it. Is eternity in The Estate all that I have to look forward to? Is that all there is for any of us? Sitting here, in the middle of the night, staring at a glowing computer screen, I am terrified that the answer to those two questions might just be yes.

Suddenly, my job at WFAC doesn't seem that bad. In fact, working there and sharing a long and healthy life with Carol feels like owning my own little slice of heaven, but I don't think that's in the cards. Tomorrow I'm going back to my doctor and I'll begin a fight against something that I don't think I'll beat. I'm thinking about going back to church, although I don't think that it will do much good.

The Estate is there, just out of sight, but it's there. I can feel it, and I can feel them, waiting for me. *You can never really leave.*

You don't find the dead. The dead find you…

…and once they do, they never, *never* let you go.

Also from Red Cape Publishing

Anthologies:

Elements of Horror Book One: Earth
Elements of Horror Book Two: Air
Elements of Horror Book Three: Fire
Elements of Horror Book Four: Water
A is for Aliens: A-Z of Horror Book One
B is for Beasts: A-Z of Horror Book Two
C is for Cannibals: A-Z of Horror Book Three
D is for Demons: A-Z of Horror Book Four
E is for Exorcism: A-Z of Horror Book Five
F is for Fear: A-Z of Horror Book Six
G is for Genies: A-Z of Horror Book Seven
H is for Hell: A-Z of Horror Book Eight
I is for Internet: A-Z of Horror Book Nine
J is for Jack-o'-Lantern: A-Z of Horror Book Ten
K is for Kidnap: A-Z of Horror Book Eleven
L is for Lycans: A-Z of Horror Book Twelve
It Came from the Darkness: A Charity Anthology
Out of the Shadows: A Charity Anthology
Castle Heights: 18 Storeys, 18 Stories
Sweet Little Chittering

David F. Gray

Short Story Collections:

Embrace the Darkness by P.J. Blakey-Novis
Tunnels by P.J. Blakey-Novis
The Artist by P.J. Blakey-Novis
Karma by P.J. Blakey-Novis
The Place Between Worlds by P.J. Blakey-Novis
Home by P.J. Blakey-Novis
Short Horror Stories by P.J. Blakey-Novis
Short Horror Stories Vol.2 by P.J. Blakey-Novis
Keep It Inside & Other Weird Tales by Mark Anthony Smith
Everything's Annoying by J.C. Michael
Six! By Mark Cassell
Monsters in the Dark by Donovan 'Monster' Smith

Novelettes:

The Ivory Tower by Antoinette Corvo

Novellas:

Four by P.J. Blakey-Novis
Dirges in the Dark by Antoinette Corvo
The Cat That Caught The Canary by Antoinette Corvo
Bow-Legged Buccaneers from Outer Space by David Owain Hughes
Spiffing by Tim Mendees
A Splintered Soul by Adrian Meredith

Novels:

Madman Across the Water by Caroline Angel
The Curse Awakens by Caroline Angel
Less by Caroline Angel
Where Shadows Move by Caroline Angel
Origin of Evil by Caroline Angel
Origin of Evil: Beginnings by Caroline Angel
The Vegas Rift by David F. Gray
The Broken Doll by P.J. Blakey-Novis
The Broken Doll: Shattered Pieces by P.J. Blakey-Novis
South by Southwest Wales by David Owain Hughes
Any Which Way but South Wales by David Owain Hughes
Appletown by Antoinette Corvo
Nails by K.J. Sargeant

David F. Gray

Art Books:

Demons Never Die by David Paul Harris & P.J. Blakey-Novis

Children's Books:

The Little Bat That Could by Gemma Paul
The Mummy Walks at Midnight by Gemma Paul
A Very Zombie Christmas by Gemma Paul
Grace & Bobo: The Trip to the Future by Peter Blakey-Novis
My Sister's from the Moon by Peter Blakey-Novis
Elvis the Elephant by Peter Blakey-Novis
Grandad, Where's Your Hair? by Tony Sands

Follow Red Cape Publishing

www.redcapepublishing.com
www.facebook.com/redcapepublishing
www.twitter.com/redcapepublish
www.instagram.com/redcapepublishing
www.pinterest.co.uk/redcapepublishing
www.patreon.com/redcapepublishing
www.ko-fi.com/redcape
www.buymeacoffee.com/redcape

Printed in Great Britain
by Amazon